Little *Red* Wagon

My Brother's Keeper

D'Aviér

Library of Congress Control Number: 2011922292

ISBN 13: 978-0-9843426-8-6
      10: 0-9843426-8-0

Cover Design: Ashley J. Long

Published by G Publishing, LLC

Printed in the United States of America

Acknowledgements

First, of course I have to give honors to my Lord & Savior for allowing this project to *finally* be finished! Father, you have blessed me with a talent that has sat idle too long. Yet, in everything you show me I also see the messages that follow shortly behind. It doesn't matter *how long* it took to get this book done, what matters most is that it's *DONE!* Thank you Jesus.

This is the page I've been looking forward to; not only because it gives me the opportunity to give thanks to those in my corner, but also because unlike other author's, it means the book is finished and this is the last page I have to type although it's first in the book. It's been a long road to get here and some of you wouldn't believe the turbulence I had to duck and dodge to get here, never-the-less, I MADE IT!

FEW who were with me during the conception of this story still remain a part of MY life and a couple are no longer a part of THIS life..... that being said, R.I.Paradise to my ex-boss, (the BEST boss I've EVER had) and my dearest friend Tracy M. Wilson. If you were still here I'd tell you how much I appreciate you standing up for me MANY TIMES when my back was against the wall, and for helping me get through the pain of the divorce. You're words of inspiration and encouragement will never be forgotten.... R.I.P to the *only* man that ever understood me, Shawn J. Guinn (Rock). I will NEVER forget our conversation the week before you left. "Never forsake your happiness for anyone." It rings in my head like bells. You'll always have a piece of my heart....until we meet again.

Ok, let me perk it up a bit because I don't want the "typical" acknowledgements! Shout out to my family: Moma & James, my sister & Brother (Tonya & Jerome), my daughters, Nika & Dasia: I will always love the two of you more than you'll ever know. I'm just as proud of you today as I was the day you were born. Always hold your heads up and never be afraid to TRY. Never settle for less than what you are worth because what you are worth is MUCH GREATER than "less" of anything! I'm not perfect, but I CAN speak from EXPERIENCE. Do as I SAY and not as I DO... I PROMISE if you throw PRAYER & FAITH in the mix.....you'll soar to boundless heights! Shout out to my little sister Iesha because we're BLOOD & the love is there.... U just gotta be willing to **accept** it. To my nephews Shay, Dionte, George, Tyree, Tyler, &Trey, my nieces: Nikki, Destiny (it's the 1st of the month!), Tierra, and Taylor I love you all.

To my sister Tonya... seems like we get closer as the years go by and even though you used to jack me up more often than not..... I love you big sister! To my brother Jerome who inspired me to do this story, Thank you big brother. I hope you & Tonya like this story..... it has a LOT of familiarity to it! You just gotta figure out where it is in the story.....Y'all gone be crackin' up!

Special shout out to my girls & homie's Snokeya Strickland, Monet Robinson-Allen, Shevonne "Shevy" Parker-Jones; Renee Chappell, Crystal Trammel, Shawnda Harris (719er), Debra "Day" Young, Misty "Michelle" Norton, Nellie Sloan, Felecia Washington, Andre "Hollywood" Young, Melvin "Men-Tal" Christian (for letting me know WHEN to end the story because I would have

STILL been typing) & Anthony Christian.....**U R MY GLUE**! Its' friends like you that God placed in my life to let me see the "REAL" me. Even though I hate when y'all flash the MIRROR OF LIFE in my face, I APPRECIATE when I see the reflection looking back at me so I can make the necessary changes to MYSELF that need to be made. With friends like y'all, I could NEVER even ATTEMPT 2 BE FAKE! Thanks for your continued support, listening ears and shoulders to cry on. You ALL always tell me what I NEED to hear and never what I WANT to hear; That's the **true** definition of a FRIEND. You all are collectively my DREAM TEAM!

Special Thanks to Mogul Minded Rein Child (719er) & Blu Out from Detroit Riot Radio (detroitriotradioonline.com) for the opportunity to be a part of one of THE hottest online radio show in the "D" and ATL. I appreciate ALL that you allowed me to be a part of and I wish you both MUCH SUCCESS! To Scottie Mac from IMM radio (http://www.immradio.com) for giving me that BOMB ASS interview with comedian Shay B, DJ Honey, Big N.O.T, & Crazy Nate....I had a BALL! Looking forward to future ventures ;-) To my manager, DJ Honey & the WHOLE Honey Management Team......LET'S GET IT! To The Video Shop on Comcast 68, thanks for believing in me & recognizing my GIFT.... I love the camera & the crew.

Thanks to all my Face Book friends: Brian Cox, Carlos Coonmeat Carter, Coonjuice (more Coonjuice please!), Carlos J. Clark, Madiha Crawford, "Joy" Rahmaan, ESG's Toya, Nisha & Tosha (y'all make me feel like a STAR), Danny Jackson (my brother ☺), King Michael Luster, De Ve Es & all the rest of y'all that "like" my statuses and "poke" me all the time! It's the little things that count. I appreciate you all for taking a chance on coming to see me perform. I'm pleased to know that you liked my pieces.

To moma & daddy; I pray that this story will SHOW you my gift of writing and shed a little light on my imagination and creativity. Thank you both for deciding to hook up the night I was conceived! I know I've had my ups and downs, but please realize that ALONG WITH those bumps and bruises came my CHARACTER. Lessons in life made me the person I am today; STRONG, GIFTED and DETERMINED to rise above what is considered average. Look at the rose & not the thorns because I have BLOSSOMED.... I owe it to you both.

A VERY special shout out to Pastor Janet Oyebode of Just for Christ Ministries. You have found a true friend in me and I am forever grateful for all the opportunities you have given me and the prayers for strength and prosperity. Thank you for opening your heart to something new like the beauty of spoken word. If you ever need anything from me, I AM HERE just like you are for me. You are truly a ray of sunshine on my cloudiest day. I LOVE YOU.

There's one more person I would like to specially thank who shall remain nameless: Thank you for your ears, shoulders & heart in my troublesome times and for holding on tight when the rollercoaster harness broke several times. It's been a bumpy ride, but I wouldn't change it for the WORLD. No matter what happens as we travel down the road of "life" or who we gain or lose along the way to *prosperity*, you will ALWAYS have my support and my heart; GENUINELY. In my Lauryn Hill voice; NOTHING

EVEN MATTERS @ ALL! No regrets; only lessons learned. Love you ☺

If I have forgotten anyone, please charge my HEAD, NOT MY HEART. I love you all and I hope that you will enjoy the contents of this novel. Nothing beats a failure but a TRY!

Last and definitely LEAST, I Gotta give a big shout out to ALL MY HATERS…. WITHOUT U, THERE WLD BE NO BETTERMENT OF SELF! In case you're not sure what I mean by that, here it is in black & white: IT'S YOU THAT MAKE ME STRIVE TO BE *THAT* MUCH BETTER!

Little Red Wagon: *My Brother's Keeper*………Enjoy!

For my brother Jerome

The Early Days

"Jeremy?" Momma called for Jeremy to take me out of the tub. She was giving me a bath and needed to go check the pork chops, fried corn, and biscuits she had frying on the stove and baking in the oven. It smelled good up in there. It was a Friday afternoon on May thirteenth of 1976, and momma was taking care of Jeremy and I by herself. Our dad passed three years ago when Jeremy and I were younger. It was hard on momma that night when she got the call about daddy being in a work related accident. Dad worked at Chrysler assembly plant for 10 years. He started working there when he was nineteen and fresh outta' high school. Momma was like a zombie for a good 3 months after she was told that one of the pressing machines at the plant came unhinged from the base of the ceiling and crushed daddy to death as he worked on the assembly line with the carburetors and spark plugs. He died instantly.

Rumor has it that even though momma settled out of court for a mere ten thousand dollars, she could have actually taken the case all the way and would have possibly received 1.5 million. A few of daddy's co-workers said they noticed that the hinges were loose when a screw hit an employee on the top of his hard hat. No one knew where the screw came from until a couple of weeks before the accident, after management told everyone in that area that the situation had been taken care of. Her lawyer tried to talk momma out of settling, but she said she just wanted it to be over with. The money was just enough to cover the cost of the funeral and pay off a few delinquent bills.

The house and two cars we had were already paid for. Daddy's "deuce and a quarter" sat in the driveway and never moved after momma was followed in it by Calvin. Calvin was one of my dad's loyal and trusted friends slash co-workers. Calvin was at our house more than his own before the accident. He was a couple of years younger than daddy and didn't have any kids. Every now and then he would stop by with a different chick in the car, but he never brought them in to meet momma. I hear that the reason he didn't was because he had the ultimate respect for my parents' marriage. Calvin was a ladies man. Momma said he didn't ever introduce her to any of his female friends because he was never with them long enough. Besides, he didn't want to bring any drama to our house. That explains why he was never home. Bricks through Calvin's windows were second nature. Momma said that over the years she and daddy had to *weed out* a few people for causing drama in their relationship. I guess Calvin didn't want to be one of those people.

Daddy got a good deal on his car. It was dark blue and had black "fluffy" dice hanging from the rear view mirror. It wasn't quite in mint condition when he bought it, but it was definitely clean. The leather interior was cream colored and the eight track radio bumped the blues. Jeremy said he always knew when dad was coming home from work because he would hear the blues blaring from the radio from a block away. Some song by a musician named "Howling Wolf" was daddy's favorite. The bumper sticker on the back of the car read: If you see a hunk, honk! Momma would be tickled when she would ride with daddy and see just how many women actually honked. Even with her in the car!

Momma's banged up green Pinto with the one white passenger door, sat neatly parked in front of the house. It was hers and daddy's first car. The same car they'd driven from grandma's house to crusade the neighborhoods they lived in after they were married. Granddad was a retired pastor. He made damn sure that my parents' got married before my daddy *slipped up!* Then it would have been a "shot gun" wedding. Daddy taught momma to drive in that car back when they *courted*, as the old folk say.

Although we stayed in one of the poorest neighborhoods in the city, our house was one of the best on the block. No lie! The frame house was painted white with green trim. Daddy painted the cement porch and iron railings the same color. Momma had it fixed up like something out of a magazine. Other neighbors would see them working in the yard or on the house and compliment them on the finished product. Of course you had those that hated, but then again, they had a valid reason to hate.

There were lounge chairs on our porch covered with floral print that matched the fresh flowers from momma's prize garden. Although the vases on the porch were mismatched, everything coordinated perfectly. Momma had all kinds of flowers that hung from the awnings covering the porch. Bees traveled by the hundreds to get a taste of the variety of pollen that encompassed the porch. We lived on McKinley between Mohawk and Vinewood in Detroit, Michigan. A few blocks from Warren and Buchanan, which were two of the roughest hoods in the city back then. There were more vacant lots on our street than houses. I think that was the reason momma took time to beautify the inside and outside of our home, because we too lived next door to a vacant lot. Our house really wasn't that big; just your typical three bedroom bungalow with one bathroom and a basement that was only big enough to fit a washer and a dryer, if we would have had a dryer.

The house was decorated pretty though. Our livin' room was peach and cream colored with hardwood floors that daddy refurbished himself. Momma had a pair of white and peach sheers entwined that served as a border around the windows with the fancy room darkener shades. It was the perfect look for a "home."

Although we didn't have a dinin' room, the kitchen was comfortable enough for us to enjoy all those bomb ass meals momma cooked on the green gas range stove. The counter tops were yellow ceramic tile that blended in perfectly with the mint green paint on the walls. The kitchen curtains were solid yellow with green and red apple print along the fancy ruffled ends. The fruit bowl patterned kitchen chairs with browns and yellows added the finishin' touches. Anyone would have thought momma was an interior decorator the way she would coordinate.

None of the second hand furniture nor appliances really matched but we had everything we needed to make our house comfortable. We even had a black and white television hooked up in the kitchen so momma could watch her stories while she cooked.

There was a garage in the back of the house, but we rarely used it unless momma was storin' old furniture or toys in it. Daddy would get mad when she would go out to the garage because he said it wasn't safe. The doors were rusted and fallin' off so daddy just had them propped up against the frame entrance of the garage. He never had a chance to get them fixed as he'd originally planned.

Momma's room was on the first floor. Her antiquated oak furniture with the fancy stuffed red pillow back headboard matched well with the glossy light grey walls. The oversized pillows that rested atop the queen size bed resembled clouds fluffed in imitation satin pillow cases that matched the sheets. For some reason, the red polka dot reversible comforter attracted Jeremy and I. We would always lay in momma's room even when daddy was here; so I've been told. I would be the first to fall asleep every time.

Momma's dresser was outlined with several family photos. She was a picture "fiend." She even had pictures jammed in a shoe box under her bed that still hadn't been developed. I would often catch her staring with a blank look on her face at pictures of her and dad at different functions. Once I walked in on her crying but she tried to play it off sayin' that she had allergies. I guess that's why she lingered with getting those other pictures developed because it hurt her to be without daddy. He was her best friend. That void would never be filled.

The artificial flowers mixed with the real plants inside the house brought life to the master bedroom. It used to be a den occupied by my parents before Jeremy and I were born. Momma and Daddy moved into it when I was able to successfully pee on my own and sleep through the night. Jeremy's and my bedrooms were on the second floor with the bathroom. The upstairs hallway was long and had the same hardwood finish as the livin' room. Jeremy's room was right at the top of the loft styled wood stained upper level, with the Victorian styled banisters. His room was white with blue accessories; lamps, comforter, pictures. There were shelves above his dresser that donned certificates and trophies proudly strewn about. Certificates of achievement and frequently polished baseball trophies were Jeremy's prize possessions. Those are the only things in life that I ever remember Jeremy holdin' *'near and dear.'* His first, second, and third baseball mitts were strategically placed between the certificates on the second shelf.

No matter how much momma offered Jeremy for an allowance to clean that "triflin" room, as she would say, it would never look the way it did when Momma used to clean it. Maybe it was before daddy died, now that I think about it. Momma used to say, "I bet it wouldn't look like this if Jeremy was here."

My room was about six feet away from Jeremy's on one side, and six feet from the bathroom on the other. Our parents liked that set up because they would check on the two of us whenever they came up the thirteen uncarpeted stairs to go relieve themselves. Momma's taste showed through the colors in my room. She loved light, soft colors; which is why daddy painted it pink and purple. There were hand painted numbers and the alphabet throughout the entire room. Daddy painted my whole room all by himself. Well, under the direction of momma, of course. The main wall in my bedroom was dressed with my name in bubble writin'. I had shelves too!

I had Barbie dolls lined up thirteen dolls deep in two rows. And let's not talk about the cars, camper, and all of my doll clothes. My dolls were so stuck up. They had everything!

None of my playmates could even bring another doll in my room if it didn't have clothes or if it had nappy hair! That was my rule because if it didn't have clothes on, that meant friends could have ended up '*slippin'* off with one of the outfits I let them borrow. And definitely 'no' to their nappy headed dolls 'cuz that meant friends would be jealous of my dolls' hair. They would end up poppin the head off their dolls, in exchange for my dolls' head. In the hood it didn't matter whether the black doll had a white head or vice versa just as long as the hair could be combed and wasn't all matted down.

Anyway, daddy did an excellent paint job on my room. He could draw his fingers off. He hooked our rooms up. Not to mention all the plastering and construction jobs he did around the house. People would actually ask daddy how much he would charge for little odds and ends around their houses. I don't know if they think daddy really needed the money or if they thought he would feel obligated to do it pro-bono since they were friends of his. But, they wrong about both. Daddy only did that home improvement stuff for us and our grandparents. Momma said he felt that if he didn't do work for them, that would be a sure way to keep the pleasant socialization goin'. He knew that the first time a person played him for his money, all lines of communication would be down! So, he alleviated the problem before it entered into existence.

From the stories I hear, daddy was very protective of me; especially in my first few weeks of life after I came home from the hospital. The neighbors were lined up at the front door to meet the 'blob' that filled momma's belly. They looked out for Jeremy and me when momma and daddy would have house projects that demanded their undivided attention. Back then the whole village was actually raising the children. If we did anything wrong or if we were anywhere *remotely* close to danger, Ms. Johnson, Pastor Eldin, and old ass Mrs. Sherry would be the ones to scold us. Mrs. Sherry was a trip. She was the woman that lived next door to us when momma and daddy first bought the house. I hear that at some point she was a nicer woman than I remember. All I ever remember was her bein' the nosiest, most sneaky, ornery ass person I have ever seen in my life. Nobody could even come close to bein' so mean! She's a whole other story, but I will tell you this: Although Mrs. Sherry would stop you from gettin' in harm's way, she would talk about yo' ass and yo' family like a dee-oh-double-gee after she saved you. Yo' momma would be all kinds of a dumb ass drunk. And, if you stepped on her grass in the process of bein' hurt, she probably wouldn't have even stopped you from gettin' hurt. She didn't play about her grass. All it took was for another neighbor to tell momma somethin' Mrs. Sherry said, and we haven't had a problem out of her since. Momma don't take nobody's mess. I learned that at an early age.

After daddy died, Jeremy took on the role as my protector. He must've picked up right where daddy left off too. He's been protectin' me for as long as I can recall callin' his name. I don't have too many memories of my dad, but he loved the mess outta' Jeremy and me from the pictures I've seen. I would get so jealous in my adolescent years when momma and Jeremy would reminisce on certain things but only because I will never see his warm, unduplicated smile anywhere other than a picture. Never will I see my father act

D'Aviér

as such the distinguished slash low-key thug gentleman I'd heard so much about. Daddy was not the "today's average guy." He was nothin' like some of these not-worthy-of-my-most-vulnerable-time, still - livin' -in- yo-momma'- basement (or attic) ass dogs out here today. His breed of male species are "few and far between" now.

From the photos, Daddy was a handsome man. He stood around 5 feet 10 inches and was a stocky build. His wavy reddish brown hair was closely cut and attributed his thick round face. The finely textured hair color complimented his smooth, caramel colored skin and dark brown eyes. The thin mustache coverin' his full set of lips was a little darker than a shadow. My daddy was a sexy man for his age. I wish he were still here makin' my momma as happy as she was on all of those pictures.

From the photos, I could tell that Jeremy looked like dad; only he was momma's complexion. Momma was sexy too, now that I think about it. She was a petite size 8 and had a bangin' ass body herself. She looked like she stepped right off the Reservation onto land and into our lives. At 145 lbs, momma didn't look like she'd given childbearing much effort. She stood 5 feet 3 inches under daddy. Her dark brown shoulder length hair drawn up in a ponytail made her hazel eyes even more noticeable in the sun. If love could be captured in a photograph, there would be millions of pictures of momma across the world. She was beautiful. Hollywood should have had a glimpse of her back then.

Jeremy and I would be so anxious to hear momma's stories about her hangin' days. It would crack us up to hear how she had to check somebody or beat somebody up back in the day. She had such a wholesome look and so much grace about herself. We couldn't believe some of the stories. What we did know was true, was that momma didn't take nobody's mess. I know I said it before, but she really didn't. I guess that was the flip side of bein' mixed with Indian. We weren't like every other black person from the hood that swore if one strand of hair laid down right, they were of Indian decent. If momma and daddy weren't full blooded, Jeremy and I were for sure. We got it from both grandmothers.

Daddy and I looked just alike; like he spit me straight outta his mouth into existence. Although I had the shape and color of momma's eyes, everything else was identical to daddy. I am the girl image of him; from the wavy hair on my head, to the narrow soles of my feet. We both had a clubbed foot (a birth defect in young children, usually infants, that makes the foot turn abnormally inward) when we were born. I used to have to wear those ugly ass blue corrective shoes that made your feet look like your shoes were on backwards. I hated those shoes! I used to hide them in the hallway closet so I wouldn't have to wear them. Wouldn't you know it? Jeremy would be the one to find them all the time. Smart ass! Well, luckily he did find them or my foot would still be that way. "Boy! I know you hear me callin' you." Momma yelled from the bathroom. She didn't want to leave me in the water by myself while she went next door and grabbed me some pajamas. I was spoiled rotten! I splashed like I was swimming in the barely bubbled water. Momma had water all on her blue jean cool locks and white lace tie up belly shirt. "Stop it Berry! You gone have water all over my floor lil' girl." I kept splashin'.

"Yes, momma?" Jeremy crept to the bathroom door unnoticed to see what momma wanted. His dark blue Wrangler jeans were crisp with starch. The pant legs came down to the white soles of his black and white Converse All Star shoes. He wore his light brown leather baseball mitt as he tossed the dingy, now yellow baseball back and forth.

"I need you to go check on my food." Jeremy cut her off. "I stirred the corn, and flipped the pork chops before I came up here. The biscuits ain't even brown." Momma smiled and said, "Well, go get Berry some night clothes out of her drawer." Jeremy obliged and turned to get the items momma requested. "Get out Berry cuz this water is startin' to get dirty." Momma grabbed the towel off the toilet seat and handed it to me to dry off as she pulled the chain to remove the rubber plug. "It's cold ma!" I shivered as I dried my legs and wrinkled feet. "Hurry up Jeremy! Get the molasses outta yo' butt boy!

Jeremy resurfaced right after I pulled up my underwear. I'd just won the wrestlin' match with my t-shirt as I struggled to get my semi-dry arm through the tee strapped shirt. He tossed me my pajamas and I raced to put them on. Now that I was outta the tub, I wanted to go downstairs and watch *Lost In Space* before momma called Jeremy in to eat. He would hog the hell outta' the TV watchin' the Dukes of Hazard. Just as I was about to make a dash towards the bathroom door, I slipped on some standing water that momma missed with the towel. "Floomp!" I fell on the floor imitating a *Prince* split; only it wasn't done intentionally. I hit my knee on the hard tile covered ceramic floor and started to cry. "Hush up girl! You wasn't gone cry until you saw me lookin'". Momma grabbed the used towel out of the hamper and dried the remaining wet spot. That's when I heard Jeremy comin' back up the stairs. I set the stage for Jeremy to rescue me. I really started cryin' then! I knew I could get the attention I needed from him. Momma used to give it to me, but I think she was on to my game. It was different with Jeremy though. With him, my cries could win an Oscar. I was truly melodramatic.

"What's wrong with Berry Ma?" Jeremy walked fast towards the bathroom to answer my distress call. I could see the concern in his worried light skinned face. He reached to help me off the floor as momma checked for any potential broken bones. "I got her Jeremy. Hush up Berry!" I was really spreadin' it on thick. Jeremy got me up off the floor. "You alright Berry?" Momma quickly interjected, "Ain't nothin' wrong with Berry Jeremy. She just wants some attention." Luckily, Jeremy didn't mind giving it to me. He walked me to my bedroom so I could get my house shoes as he wiped my tears.

Head 2 Head

By the time I turned 11, Jeremy was every bit of a headed for trouble sixteen. That's when momma started to really pounce on Jeremy's ass about his school work and declining grades. Jeremy was a smart student, but for some odd reason he wasn't focused anymore. At one point it mattered to Jeremy if he got a 'C' instead of a 'B' on his school work. Momma got calls from the school almost every other day about Jeremy's behavior. She swore that they had our number on speed dial. He was constantly gettin' kicked out for fightin'.

I remember one night at the dinner table, momma told Jeremy to take out the trash after dinner. He looked at her and rolled his eyes, but momma didn't see it though. As we continued to eat, I guess momma noticed that Jeremy had barely touched his food. "Eat your vegetables Jeremy." Momma was a firm believer that a vegetable had to be cooked with every meal for physical and mental growth. "For what? I ain't no kid." Jeremy was bein' sarcastic as hell with momma. I remembered thinkin' to myself, "This boy must be outta his mind!" I started to slowly ease away from the table 'cuz I just knew a fist was about to be thrown in Jeremy's direction. I'd never seen my brother act like this or be defiant towards momma. My heart was beatin' a hundred beats per minute and my eyes started to water.

"What did you just say?" As if she didn't comprehend Jeremy's remarks, momma had a look of disbelief on her face like, "Did he just say what I think he said?" He had a chance to redeem himself; take it all back and start over anew. But instead he replied, "I said, I ain't no kid." My eyes were ten times their normal size. I already knew what was next so I just started cryin'. I knew that Jeremy was about to get the all-time ass kickin' of his life.

"Now see what you did? You made Berry cry." Momma leaped up from the table and got straight in Jeremy's face. Her face was so close to his, that while she screamed their lips touched a couple of times. "I don't know who you *think* you're talkin' to in that tone young man, but I will bust your fuckin' lip if you *ever*, and I do mean *ever* Jeremy, talk to me like that again. Do you understand me?" Jeremy sat there with his chair on two legs tryin to lean out of momma's face. He was scared to move. He knew for sure that momma had her limit with him and his attitude. Of all the times she let him slide, today would not be one of those days. Momma balled her fist and asked Jeremy, "So, what you wanna do now tough ass? You wanna fight me?" Jeremy lowered his chair and mumble "naw" under his breath. By this time I'd been cryin' so hard that snot was running down my lip. I begged, "No momma, No! Please momma!" She stayed in that same spot starin' Jeremy in his eyes without even blinkin'. "If you think you wanna fight me boy, then you can find your own house. In this house you will obey me until the day I die. You got that? I will beat yo' ass if you ever talk to me in that tone again." Momma finally backed away. "Go wash your face Berry!" I knew not to think about it too long or I would be next. I ran up the stairs to the bathroom and got cleaned up.

As I made my way back downstairs, I heard the front door slam. I guess Jeremy was upset that momma hurt his man pride; or boy pride. What really shocked me was that momma didn't even try to stop him. I started helpin' her clear the dinner table. Momma grabbed the bowl with the three uneaten biscuits and started to cry. This was the second time in my entire life that I'd seen momma cry.   The first time was when she said she had allergies after I sneaked up on her lookin' at pictures of daddy.   I started cryin' with momma.   It hurt me so bad to see how Jeremy broke my mother down.   She was tryin' her hardest to make a way for the two of us by ironing people's clothes, babysittin', and cleanin' people's nasty ass houses.   Even though the houses she cleaned were church members that knew us and just wanted to help out.   Nevertheless, some of those people were just nasty ass people.   You wouldn't believe the things my mother would come across cleanin' up somebody's filth. Dirty sanitary pads left behind the toilets, sheets with blood or shit stains embedded in them.   She said once she cleaned an elderly ladies bedroom and found used condoms and sex toys.   Momma said she was so embarrassed, but the lady didn't seem to be bothered by it at all. She did all of that for Jeremy and me. All so she wouldn't have to ask nobody for nothin'.

"It's aw'right momma."   I wiped her red eyes with some of the unused portion of the tissue I got from upstairs. "I do whatever I can for y'all Berry. And look how Jeremy is actin'. He act like I deserve to be treated like this!"   She continued to replay the incident in her head as the tears flowed down her flawless cheeks.   I gave momma the tissue while I continued to clean off the table and prepare dish water.   I couldn't believe my eyes; my mother at her weakest moment. I stood there washin' dishes.   For some reason I thought about how momma must've really been tired of all the crap Jeremy, and occasionally me, would put her through. I'd only been chastised by her a couple of times myself. I remember the one time I underestimated momma and I got straight up *'whooped'* and punished for actin' like my ass was on my shoulders. Momma told me I couldn't go outside. What did she say that for? I started cryin' and stompin' around the house. I think I may have even slammed a door or two. Momma told me to come to her and I acted like I didn't hear her. "Come here right now Berry!"

Stubborn me; I was gone show her that she was gone let me go outside, or I was gone be pissed with her for the rest of the day. The second part of that sentence was right; 'cuz I was pissed for the rest of the day. Pissed and bruised up. Momma came and grabbed me after she commanded me to come to her. But, I was so mad that I yanked my arm away from her. That was one ass kickin' I will never forget. Even if I never get another one, I'll never forget that one. She whooped me with a switch she made me pick off the neighbors magnolia tree. I ended up pickin' one of the ones that wasn't quite brown with bark, but kinda green like. Not yet a branch, but more like a limb. Please! I had welts on my body for three days. I never looked at the tree the same after that. How could somethin' that looked so pretty and smelled so good, turn out to be a weapon of mass destruction?

Momma ended up cryin' herself to sleep. Before she retired for the night, I took her some Tylenol to calm down the headache she complained about. She was still cryin' as she took off her clothes and put on her long pink nightgown. I couldn't help but to feel sorry for her. I was furious with

Jeremy, but more so because it was his week to do the dishes!

Jeremy's ass didn't creep in the house until four hours later. "Where's momma Berry?" Jeremy whispered as he crept in the kitchen, right past momma's room. I ignored him. "Berry? Is momma awake?" He tried to switch the question up a bit as if he didn't notice my silence towards him. "Do you see her anywhere?" I snapped and smacked my lips. "Naw she ain't awake. I hope you're happy you made her cry stoo-ped!" He stood there lookin' dumbfounded. I guess he couldn't believe that his 'lil Berry was mad at him.

"Don't you start that! I feel bad enough without being reminded. Man, she just made me mad Berry. I'm tired of her treatin' me like a 'lil boy. I get tired of her having to iron people's clothes and clean people's nasty ass houses. If dad was here she wouldn't even have to work. I cut him off out of anger. "Well, daddy isn't here! How can you be tired of momma workin' and makin' a livin' for *us*? She does everything for us Jeremy. You need to ask God to forgive you." Jeremy grabbed me by my arm. In all the years I've known him, he'd never done anything harmful to me. But the look in his eyes tonight told a different story.

I started to cry again. "Shhhhh. Listen Berry," he tried to calm me down. I could tell that he'd actually snapped out of his trans or whatever it was that had him grippin' my arm like that. "Momma doesn't have enough money to keep this house and take care of us. Daddy left us money Berry, but momma used it all payin' the bills and tryin' to keep a roof over our heads. Daddy always told me that I would be the man of the house if anything happened to him." Tears started to form in Jeremy's eyes as his voice started to squeak.

All I could think was, "Not you too." I'd had enough tears and nose blows for one night. My brother was strong and I didn't want to see him like this. I grabbed his waist and hugged him as tight as I could. He gripped my wrists and pushed me back. "Berry? Man, you just don't know." I was frustrated with the mixed emotions he displayed. "What Jeremy?" He walked to the kitchen sink for a drink of water. He talked to me with his back turned. "You're too young to understand," he said as he drank out of the blue tumbler cup I'd just washed.

I just sat there with a confused look on my face. I was flustered because not just ten minutes ago, Jeremy just told me that he was tired of momma treatin' him like a little boy. Yet here he is tellin' me I'm too young to understand. If he was tired of hearin' it, then how much longer would it be before he would realize that I didn't want to hear that shit either? He turned to me and reached in his pocket as I sat at the table with my hand on my chin. "You may not understand this, but I found it on the dining room table. We about to be on the street Berry."

I took the paper out of the envelope marked 'Urgent!' When I unfolded the top part of the letter, the word FORECLOSURE stood out in bold red letters. There were numbers and dates on the paper, but it really didn't mean much to me. "What is this Jeremy? What does this mean?" "Momma is about to lose this house Berry. She missed the last two payments on the house. According to this, she took out another mortgage on the house. That's probably how she bought us all that stuff for school. Plus the furnace went out last winter. I was talkin' to Andre down the street when his dad took us with him to get a new hot water tank. Mr. Nelson said it was expensive to get a hot water tank and a furnace costs even more."

Jeremy was so overwhelmed by all of the current events that had taken place. For some reason he felt like momma should have told him and he could have possibly resolved her financial strains. I failed to understand how he could have helped her. It wasn't like he had a job! Hell, the paper route he had two years ago only lasted for about three months. Just long enough for momma to realize that the manager, Mr. Banks, was rippin' Jeremy off. Jeremy delivered papers to three blocks around the neighborhood. Pullin' his wagon and throwin' all those newspapers after school. When it came to collecting money owed, the customers' wouldn't even answer the doo!. The ones' that did would tell Jeremy to come back tomorrow or next week. For every dollar Jeremy didn't collect, Mr. Banks deducted three dollars from his pay. Some weeks Jeremy would come home with a whole ten dollars for the week!

"Berry, if momma don't come up with fifteen hundred dollars in thirty days, we gone have to move somewhere else. I ain't gone let that happen Berry!" Jeremy raised his voice angrily at the thought of us having to move. I couldn't understand why he kept sayin' we would be on the "streets." After all, our grandparents didn't stay too far from us. I asked him, "What about grandma and grandpa Jeremy? They won't make us stay out on the streets. We can go there!" I thought I'd found a resolution to the problem, but that only seemed to make Jeremy more agitated. He shot my idea down like a unknown enemy jet crossing into and unauthorized area. Little did I know, our grandparents were strict on momma as a child. Seems that Jeremy overheard momma tellin' somebody in casual conversation how she would never burden my grandparents by goin' back home and livin' with them. Apparently, Ms. Sherry, our nosey neighbor suggested that momma sell the house and move back with her parents after daddy died.

"Jeremy continued his tantrum, "I promised dad that I would look after you and momma if anything happened to him. I ain't about to let us get put out!" I looked at the paper again to see if I could decipher any of the writin' into plain English; to no avail though. "What you gone do Jeremy?" I asked like I was ready for a response or an action plan. I was even willin' to give up my fifteen dollars in nickels and dimes to contribute to the cause. I was dyin' to spend it anyway! Momma wouldn't let me spend it on candy like I wanted to, so I know she wouldn't mind me givin' it to her to help keep the house.

"You want my money Jeremy?" I was all too excited to show momma that I was responsible enough to help. I don't know why it meant so much to me, but I guess in my own way, I wanted to prove to momma that I was old enough to handle things too. Jeremy turned down my offer. "Naw, you keep your money Berry. I'm gone have it by the time it's due."

Jeremy looked more serious than I'd seen him look; like when he'd be at home base concentratin' on hittin' a fast ball. He was truly dedicated to momma and me. He hung on to every last word he and dad had. I think he was more so concerned about me and momma then he was about himself. "I ain't about to let none of us be on the streets Berry. I

D'Aviér

won't let that happen."

He walked towards momma's room to check on her. "Come on Berry, let's go upstairs and go to bed." He whispered in a weary tone. Jeremy's anxiety was obvious. "I'll apologize to momma in the morning." Although Jeremy didn't have so much as a paper route, I knew he wasn't gone let momma down. He meant what he said about savin' our house. No matter what he had to do; whatever it took.

From that point on my brothers' and my relationship grew tighter than ever. He confided in me about anything he felt he couldn't trust anyone else with. Although I was younger than him, my male sibling looked at me as if I were his equal from that night on. We were tight like Krazy Glue on bare skin. My brother would do anything for me and vice versa. It remained that way for the rest of our lives.

Message

The economic crisis that my city and state face makes me contemplate;
Like a game of chess I try to strategize my next move.
Fantasizing the about winning this game we call "life" as I face the blatant truth,
That this economy is not equipped for me and I'm stripped of my beliefs and dreams;

All because the government expresses no means for my existence. My soul screams!
Ignored like a plague or rare epidemic; monetarily and socially disgraced.
Because I'm falling to my knees and can't seem to keep up the pace,
But my faith; the one thing that can't be touched, although it's constantly poked and probed
My will to maintain longevity, peace and control; my struggles waiver
As He continues to hold my hand; helping me stand firm on a foundation; one without stacks of paper.
Only He knows the content of my heart and accepts me for who I am; HE is MY Savior.

And so I stand with grace, dignity and pride as I continue to strive to make a change.
Even though I am falling, He grabs a net because in this struggle I call out His name.

D'Aviér

The answer to my problems is to simply, "Just be patient."
You see, it's not just about ME and MY livelihood, this
problem spreads all across our nation.

My gratification comes from taking that chance; believing in
His power and stepping out on my faith.
It is now that I realize He would never leave me or allow me
to fall flat on my face.
The taste of victory is near, although I worry about "When?"
I have no fears.
As I'm comforted and spoken to spiritually, "Just be ready
when your many blessings appear!"
Now tell me, is this a message that only I am able to hear; or
to others is this message clear?

~ D'Aviér

Pocket Change

It's now day fifteen of the thirty that momma was given to come up with the money to save our home. Jeremy had been in and out of the house for the past few weeks. The calls from school eventually ended and momma had become accustomed to seeing Jeremy home at different times of the day. It was obvious that he'd dropped out. Surprisingly, the truant officers' stopped comin' after the first few weeks. Jeremy resigned his student position at the neighborhood high school. Momma continued to do her ironing and cleanin'. Only now, her cleanin' had been reduced to just our house. She never said it, but I know she quit cleaning other houses because she wanted to keep a close eye on Jeremy.

When I came home from school, momma and Jeremy were sittin' in the car in front of the house. Momma was in good spirits, quite the opposite of the past moods she'd been in. Her headaches seemed to be comin' more frequently now, but the Tylenol she bought bi-weekly seemed to keep her pain in check. "Get in Berry." Jeremy lifted his seat so I could climb in. His brand new Levis and unwrinkled Adidas shirt were neat and coordinated along with his pure white leather Adidas high top sneakers. "Where we 'bout to go?", I asked curiously.

"To get some food after I pay the gas and water bills." Momma must have made a lot of money this week. She was happy and carefree like her normal self again. She didn't seem to have a worry in the world at this point. We continued to head towards the local grocery store, four blocks down off Buchanan.   It was the Wednesday before the Fourth of July and momma was shopping for the feast she would prepare for us.

As we walked up and down the aisles, Jeremy and I grabbed a few of our favorite items and threw them in the basket. Momma would put them back on the shelf when we weren't lookin'; we were too preoccupied with the next items we sneaked into the almost half full buggy. When momma bent down to grab a bag of flour from the bottom shelf in the pancake and brownie isle, she bumped into the man standin' across from her. He was bent over price comparin' vegetable oils.

"Excuse me!" They both said it simultaneously. The five foot nine inches, medium brown man with the finely groomed goatee looked into momma's eyes and began to smile. "A woman as pretty as you can bump into me anytime!" Momma blushed and apologized again. Jeremy was busy checkin' out what type of Pop Tarts he wanted. He turned to ask me which kind I wanted when he saw the forbidden, unauthorized flirtation. Jeremy's whole facial expression changed as he tossed the box of pastries back on the shelf by the oatmeal.

"So, you need help carrying your food to your car? My Cadillac is parked close to the door." The look on his face showed he had other things on his mind as he looked momma up and down. Her halter top displayed her finely perched breast, which his eyes frequented. "She's straight! Our car is parked at the front door." Jeremy lied and interrupted before momma could turn down the offer. Jeremy walked up with his chest stuck out. It was like somethin' out of the movies; like when something would happen and you could hear the needle scratch across the '45? He stood in front of momma to block the strangers' view of momma's physique. "Jeremy! Momma talked through her teeth without movin' her lips as she often did when one of us irritated the hell out of her. "Stop being rude!" She apologized for Jeremy's disrespectful behavior. "Awww! That's o.k. sweetheart. He's just lookin' out for his mother. I would do the same thing if my mom was as fine as you." At this time I wasn't quite sure if he was complimenting my mother or insultin' his own. Jeremy didn't care either way as he continued to grim the man out; lookin' him in his eyes without blinkin' nor flinchin'. He stayed posted by momma's side like he was her hired security. "You ready ma?"

Jeremy grabbed the buggy and motioned for me to start walkin' down the aisle.

"Come on Jeremy! Let me grab some eggs for my macaroni and cheese." She rolled her eyes and turned back to the man with the Cadillac. "Thanks again for the offer sir, but we're fine."

Momma and I proceeded to walk to the end of the isle. I noticed that Jeremy wasn't behind us. Momma wasn't payin' attention. She was probably glad that she didn't have to show her true colors with Jeremy. Maybe she was just glad that she got through those weak ass advances from the stranger. Jeremy stood toe to toe with the man that made passes at momma. Even though he wasn't the man's height, he stood there grimacing and flinching like he could look the man eye to eye. I remember I kind of chuckled and momma pinched the back of my arm. Jeremy just looked so funny standin' there. He was really testin' his manhood; just like the tribe of lion cubs on the nature channel. His piercin' look went right through the man. He never even considered that he was bein' disrespectful to an adult. Momma didn't play when it came to kids being disrespectful to elders. The man just looked Jeremy up and down with a smirk on his face. He sucked his teeth and mumbled, "You remind me of myself when I was your age young man." Jeremy didn't acknowledge the comment. Finally, the man sucked his teeth and walked away.

The whole thing happened so fast. I mean, before momma's mind could even register the thought that she was bein' hit on, Jeremy was on her like a coyote on a roadrunner. Now that I think about it, Jeremy didn't even blink or stumble over his words. I don't think he cared that momma could have smacked his lips on the floor for steppin' out of a "child's place."

Momma finished shoppin' by grabbin' a few of her last minute items. From the looks of the basket, she wasn't too worried about losin' our house. Anyone would have thought that we were well off by all the food in our grocery cart. There was even some of the sweets that Jeremy and I had sneaked in......again while momma wasn't lookin'. As we approached the cashier at the checkout line, the Arabian woman dressed in a blue smock looked at us like she was disgusted by our overflowin' items. Or maybe it was because of the argument she'd just concluded with the old lady in front of us tryin' to purchase more cat food than the store coupon allowed. Either way, the rude cashier sighed loudly and rang up our stuff.

The total of the bill was one hundred ten dollars and fifty eight cents. I remember momma looking in her purse for the manila envelope she reused whenever she had a lump sum of money. Only Jeremy and I knew about the envelope. Momma was careful not to pull it completely outta her purse. She only counted out what she needed. "Here's fifty dollars on that ma." Did I just see and hear what I think I heard? It was Jeremy pullin' out a lump of dollar bills and a twenty and ten flashed by. "I got it Jeremy. And where did you get that money from?" Momma handed the clerk the money and waited for Jeremy's response. The teenaged girls standin' behind Jeremy started smilin' and whisperin' to each other. They were too obliged to happen to be there to hear Jeremy's response. The minute we walked down aisle five, they were both followin' behind Jeremy, actin' silly and shit. It was probably safe to assume that their nosey asses saw Jeremy's episode a couple of isles ago.

"Mr. Potts let me cleanup for him after the barber shop closes. I've been working for him for about a couple of months." Jeremy was searchin' for a date as the lie rolled off his tongue. The dusty ass girls behind him started to giggle. "That's were I've been going every day. The lies continued as Jeremy set the stage to make up for unaccounted time he spent away from home. He was quick on his feet. Even though the barber shop was on the corner of Buchanan, momma never took the time to walk those two blocks since Jeremy was around seven or eight. She started lettin' Jeremy go on his own around the age of eight or nine. She said Jeremy was old enough and that she was teachin' him responsibility by lettin' him go on his own. That was back when it really did take a village to raise a child. Everybody on the block knew the McDaniel family. Our name was proudly spoken in that area. Mr. Potts used to cut daddy's hair too. He was another adopted "relative" momma and daddy took a likin' to. We eventually started callin' him 'uncle Preston; by his first name.

"Well, as long as you doin' something positive, since school ain't in your schedule." Momma put Jeremy on front. One of the girls all in our business had a frown on her face when she heard the statement momma made. The one with the tight Levis and blue tube top looked like she was impressed. Her feathered haircut was fluffy and shiny from the half pound of grease she packed in it. Her dingy grey tennis shoes that once read Reebok, now read Ree ok! How the hell did the 'b' wear off? She was definitely lookin' for attention. The minute she noticed that Jeremy had actually noticed the two them lookin'; the games began.

Jeremy looked embarrassed, but maintained his coolness. "So, you don't want it ma? Jeremy offered the money to momma again. This time when she refused it, a female's voice said, "I want it!" My mouth dropped. I turned to look at momma to see if she heard it. She was turned facin' the cart as the bagger loaded an empty cart with our groceries. I know she heard it. Why didn't she say anything? Jeremy stayed behind as momma summoned me to come on. I heard him ask her name. Uuuugh! I can't believe he's talkin' to her. I couldn't stand the thought of my brother talkin' to her. "Come on Jeremy!" I yelled when momma and I reached the automatic doors. Momma put the grocery bill and change in her loosely stitched pocketbook she kept tucked in her bra. "Thank you Jesus!" She praised God as we reached the parkin' lot. By then Jeremy caught up to help unload the groceries. "If it wasn't for the church helpin' us out with the mortgage this month, I don't know what I would have done."

That explains why Jeremy and I had to wait after church with sistah Beulah and her six bad ass absent-parent kids. They ranged from age eighteen to thirteen. She had two sets of twins. Momma went to talk one on one with Pastor Elkins and a few other members of the congregation at Mt. Holy Temple Baptist Church on Woodrow Wilson and Taylor. Sistah Beulah was one of the church members that belonged to the church before I was born. She sang annoyingly in the choir and was a member of the Usher Board along with two of her six children. The oldest girls, Tirianna and Twanna, were identical twins. I never could understand how they could look exactly alike; yet one was beautiful and the other was a beast. Twanna was only a few minutes older than Tirianna, but she was so nice and smiled all the time. She wore conservative clothes to church and always spoke to everyone. Tirianna had scratches on her face that were slightly faded out over the years. Her hair was always full of gel and grease slicked back into a tacky ponytail. Her Sunday dresses were what she'd been seen in at neighborhood clubs the night before.

The middle children, Damon and Lynette, were fourteen and fifteen. They were very manner able and smart as hell too. Damon was a spelling bee champion in middle school. He looked just like sistah Beulah. Lynette was a mathematician. She could calculate math faster than the teacher could finish writin' the problem on the board. She must have looked like her dad; whoever he was. She was a medium brown complexion with a decent grade of hair. I guess Tirianna used to do her hair because she always wore her hair slicked to the back too. She just didn't require as much gel as her big, nasty attitude sister.

Myron and Mitchell were sistah Beulah's 'babies'. They were the last set of twins and the most beautifully created boys I'd ever seen! They looked like two well-based turkey and dressin' dinners on Thanksgiving day. Ummm, Ummm! Mouthwaterin' good. It was rumored that their daddy was an Italian guy named Giovante Perelli. He owned a tire shop off Tireman and Livernois in Detroit. Some of the elderly shit starters in church would joke that if it rained for more than an hour one day, sistah Beulah would be pregnant by the time it stopped! Her ex-husband Paul ran up in her like it was his job. As a matter of fact, he stayed up in her more than he actually worked. He ran off with a woman he met in the butcher shop over on Vinewood.

It wasn't too long after Paul left that sistah Beulah started playing bed tag with Giovante Perelli. People around the neighborhood ridiculed him for hittin' some black ass. Every now and then he would pick up Damon and Lynette and take them to Edgewater Park with him, Myron and Mitchell. He never married sistah Beulah like she would often tell people, but he took care of his kids by her. He never missed his late night Tuesday and Thursday creep either. After the shop closed, it wouldn't be too long before we would see his black Lincoln with the dented door pullin' up in front of their house. He always had a brown paper bag with something' in it. Jeremy said it was probably some liquor.

I wanted to go to church every Sunday just to see Myron and Mitchell. Mitchell was mischievous, he stayed into everything. He was always gettin' in trouble for rubbin' a girls leg, or feelin' on somebody's butt. His mannish ways could have landed him at the top of a sexual harassment list. His name would stand out like a sore thumb. It seems a lot of girls thought he was just as fine as I felt Myron was. Of course; they *were* identical,except for their attitudes.

Myron was the polite one. He treated me like I was one of his boyz. We would play with his remote control trucks and crash them into each other. We used to play red light, green light while we waited for Sunday school to start. One day before church, he even played jacks with me. He sucked at it too, but it was just the fact that he didn't care how people would look at him. When Jeremy took a bathroom break, Myron and I played tag through the church's hallway. I enjoyed spendin' time with him. Everything was goin' fine until Mitchell, the "evil" twin, stuck his leg out and made me crash to the floor. I busted my bottom lip. My dress flew up in the back to reveal my blue and white cotton panty wedgie. I was so damned embarrassed that I just started to cry out of humiliation. Mitchell was tickled by my stuntman fall. So much, that he drew even more attention to me by laughin' than I did by cryin'. Within a matter of minutes, a crowd started to form around me. I did manage to take care of my wedgie before I was made a spectacle of. I remembered lookin' to see if Myron was one of the laughin' onlookers. He wasn't though. He asked me if I was alright and extended his right hand to me. He was so sweet.

Myron lifted the yellow remote control car and hit Mitchell in the head. Not hard, but just enough to get his point across. He was so mad at his brother that he was ready to 'go-to-blows' with the mirror image of himself. "Man, that ain't funny! Why you trippin' people? Myron raised his deepening voice at Mitchell. Still laughin', Mitchell held his head in the stingin' spot where the remote racecar landed. "It was funny man!"

That's it Mitchell! I'm puttin' yo' butt in a boy's home." Sistah Beulah hollered from across the church pew as she came runnin' through the crowd while Myron helped me off the floor. "Tirianna! Run to the nurses' station and get me a cold rag so I can put it on Berry's lip." She ordered the youngest twin girl to assist her. "Shush up Berry! You gone have yo' momma thinking Mitchell tried to kill you. Hush up before she come back. You ain't 'bout to die."

Tirianna, the ugliest of the twins, disappeared from my cryin' eyes to accommodate her mother's request. She was the one I heard a couple of church members sayin' would be the first to make sistah Beulah a grandmother. They went on to say that Tirianna had been caught in a car havin' sex with an old man from the barber shop. The windows were foggy and all they could see were handprints and the car bouncin' up and down. When the breath stained windows cleared, Tirianna allegedly got out of the car with one hand extended. She buttoned her blouse and straightened her skirt with the other. After she was paid for services rendered, the man in the green Pontiac sped off. Yup, left her right there by the curb where she met him.

By the time Tirianna returned with the rag, the crowd of spectators had moved on. Jeremy was comin' back from the bathroom with another boy from our church named DeAngelo. ""Angelo was about fifteen and was the 'go to' man whenever somethin' happened around the hood. He'd been marked as a troubled teen. But even with the mark of the black sheep, he was in church every Sunday with his grandmother. Except when he was incarcerated in the Wayne County Youth Home on East Forest and Chrysler. He always had on the newest tennis shoes and gear. His grandma took good care of him, or so people thought. She never held conversations with any of the other congregation. Ms. Beldon was a jazzy grandma. She always wore fancy suits and hats to church. Her accessories included a diamond bracelet with the matchin' earrings. She was a heavy set dark complexioned woman. Everything about her said "money." She would come to church before service so she could get as close to the altar as she could. When Pastor Elkins said somethin' that hit 'home' she clapped and yelled "Halleluah! Preach on!"

Ms. Beldon knew all of the church hymns too. She would sing along wavin' her gold and diamond filled hand in the air. But after service, she was gone; nowhere to be seen. There was no socializin', shakin' hands, nor eatin' in the basement of the church.

Jeremy ran towards me and my distress call. He yanked the rag out of Tirianna's hand and grabbed me away from sistah Beulah. "What happened?" Sistah Beulah quickly responded in an effort to shift the blame from Mitchell. "It was an accident Jeremy. Berry and Myron was runnin' all around here, and Mitchell made a mistake and tripped Berry." There was a pause in my act. Myron and I both interjected at the same time. "That wasn't no accident!" Myron chimed in, "He did that on purpose. You always takin' up for Mitchell ma." I continued my dramatic cry where I left off. Jeremy put the cold rag on my lip. I knew my bother loved me and at times I played on it. Although Jeremy probably knew he was my spawn, there was never a time he wasn't there for me. I was the only one that could use him like that.

After the commotion, when my last squeezed out tear dried and the single drop of blood on my lip vanished, momma reappeared from the double doors that concealed the church's conference room. There wasn't any evidence left for me to provide an "encore" scene. She walked carefree down the carpeted middle aisle towards the pew Jeremy and I sat waitin' in. Pastor Elkins and one other member of the congregation followed shortly behind. "Thank you and the congregation so much for your generosity Pastor.

My family and I are blessed to belong to this church family. I know that if my husband were still alive today, he would be grateful for all the church has done for us. Especially in our time of need." Momma was emotional as she spoke to the pastor while shakin' his hand. "Sistah Brandy, God has made a way for you and your family in your time of need. He did so through the congregation. If it weren't for the tithes and donations provided through the congregation, there would be no church standing here today. If there is ever a time that you need me or the congregation, please don't hesitate. Brotha Jeremy, God rest his soul, was a good man in the church and the community. The congregation and I are honored that we could be of assistance to your family." He spoke like a politician canvassin' for votes.

Momma wiped her tear filled eyes as the pastor said goodbye to Jeremy and I. Jeremy looked a little relieved after eaves dropping on the conversation. We both hoped that the church's donation would somehow save us from being put out on the street. Before we left, Jeremy made sure he made his presence known to Mitchell, who was still laughin' about my fall as we approached the door to leave the church. If I know Jeremy like I do, Mitchell wouldn't be laughin' for long.

Gone Be Alright

-

Although life situations seem to knock me down,
And I struggle to get back to solid ground with all my might
Once I finally regain my balance I tell myself that
I'm gone be alright

-

Things may get out of hand; as I'm slipping my grip holds
tight
I take control; success is not a privilege but a MUST in this
life
And even if it takes a few tries my faith says,
"I'm gone be alright"

-

People enter and leave through a revolving door
Those who truly aren't meant to be forever take flight
But once I re-strategize it's then that I realize that
I'm gone be alright

-

No longer blinded by deception and turmoil
My eyes are opened wider giving me unlimited sight
As I look towards the sky; I now see the big picture
I'm gone be alright

-

My struggles are ending; these battles I no longer waive life to
fight
Headaches start to diminish; I now sleep better at night
I dust off the haters, hurt, pain and anger
My eyes are open wide; not even the darkest cloud can blur
my sight

I know for certain stormy winds still occur on days that are
bright
But for as long as I am blessed to see another tomorrow, I
know that
I'm gone be alright!

~*D'Aviér*

B.D.D.S (boyz doin' dumb sh**)

As we continued to put the last few bags in the car, I ran around the car attemptin' to reach the front seat before Jeremy. "I got front Jeremy!" Jeremy slammed the hatchback on the car once the last bag was loaded. "Quit playin' Berry! You know my legs too long for the back seat." I locked the door so he couldn't get in. Just as momma was about to open the door with her key, a horn blew. Bomp Bommmp! It was sistah Beulah pullin' up in the parkin' lot. "Hey sistah Brandy!" She waved to get momma's attention. "Hello sistah Beulah." Momma yelled across the parkin' lot where sistah Beulah parked her clean light blue '78 Buick Skyhawk. Sistah Beulah opened the car door and adjusted the bucket seat for one of the kids to get out of the car. Damon squeezed out of the back seat, afro first. He was much taller than the last time I'd seen him. Over the summer he and Lynette had been livin' with their grandmother. "Hey sistah Brandy." Damon spoke to momma as he waited for the money so he could run into the store for his mother. I noticed the passenger door open. My eyes were delighted with the sight! It was Myron! I started grinnin' like I was about to take a pre-school picture.

Just as my gratification was building, I realized the sneaky smirk on Myron's face. "That's not Myron, that's Mitchell!" My smile was now a disgusted frown. Jeremy's neck twisted like he was possessed when he heard me yell out Mitchell's name. He'd wrestled me into the back seat with the groceries. It was my first claustrophobic experience. "I can't stand that nigga!" Jeremy had an even more abhorring look on his face than I did. He didn't take his eyes off Mitchell from that point; staring him up and down. I have to admit, Mitchell looked good in that red Puma sweat suit with the matching tennis shoes. He wore his straight hair cut close and tapered around the sides. A shadow of hair covered his top lip. His Italian features were definitely evident today for some reason. I guess I just never took the time to really look at Mitchell, but he was clearly just as fine as Myron. I wondered where Myron was, but I was too busy being nosey listenin' to Momma and sistah Beulah's conversation. Mitchell spoke, hugged momma, and followed behind Damon.

Sistah Beulah told momma that she'd been tryin' to get in touch with her and had just left our house before she came to the grocery store. "Sistah Brandy? Damon wanted to know if he could come to your house and wait for the guy that sells the fireworks to come home? I have to go to the clinic to pick up Tirianna. She called me and said I have to come and speak with the physician before they'll treat her. Sistah Beulah leaned in and started whisperin' something to momma.

"I hope she ain't askin' momma if her kids can come over." Jeremy talked like he was the man of the house. As if momma had to get his approval before she could do somethin. "I can't stand them look- a-like punks." I was offended that he had anything to say about Myron. Especially in the same negative sentence that he used Mitchell's name. "Myron ain't even with them Jeremy." I said it with authority as I rolled my eyes and shook my head simultaneously. I don't know why Jeremy was mad at Myron anyway. He didn't do anything to me.

"So what!" He shouted at me spittin' in my face. "If they come over I'm fuckin' them both up. Myron ain't gone let nothin' happen to his brotha'. If Mitchell comes over *with* or *without* Myron, I'm kickin' his ass. He don't be embarrassin' you in church and makin' you cry."
That's when I let him have it. I was rolling my eyes and twisting my neck so much I thought I'd sprained it. "Fo' yo' information Jeremy, Myron was the one that helped me pull my dress down. And he helped me up off the floor. You wasn't even there! You was gone with Angelo." There I was defending Myron to Jeremy and Jeremy was lookin' out for me. I screamed at the top of my lungs until my face turned red.

"Whatever Berry! Like I said, let 'em come to our house and see what happens." Just like that. It was the end of the conversation and I couldn't come up with anything better than, "That's why you ugly and you stank!" I *had* to have the last word and with Jeremy, I always did.

Momma opened the door before Jeremy could say anything else. "O.k., I'll see you in a minute. You can just follow me to the house when the boys come outta the store." Oh well, I thought to myself. Looks like Mitchell is about to get his butt kicked. Well, at least Myron wasn't with him. I sighed with relief.

After we helped momma unpack the groceries, she gave us her 'Brandy-seal-of-approval' to go outside. We called it that because she would check our rooms and each chore we were assigned to make sure they were to her liking. Jeremy was often late meetin' with friends because his room was usually junky as hell. He would throw clothes under his bed or stuff them in the closet. You would think that after he knew momma caught on, he would stop or at least switch it up. This wasn't the case.

Mitchell ended up goin' with sistah Beulah and Damon was the one that stayed with us. Jeremy and Mitchell caught eyes. Although they didn't speak to each other, they didn't fight either. Mitchell had no idea that he was going to be attacked if he'd stayed. I wasn't quite sure of Jeremy's perception of Damon, but they seemed to hit it off quite well. I guess because Damon was so quiet and polite, Jeremy really didn't consider him a threat; unlike he felt about Damon's younger brother.

"Ain't no girls over here man?" Damon spoke with a deep tone and a smirk on his face; his dark brown eyes glaring in the sun. Man, all the females is about four blocks over by the playground. They go there to watch the dudes play ball." Jeremy was all too eager to respond. "So, what we waitin' on?" Jeremy smiled at Damon's question and they went off walkin'. Sistah Beulah had only been gone for about twenty minutes and momma was in the kitchen tryin' to figure out what she was gone cook for dinner today. She had a nice selection of meats to choose from.

"Berry? What you want for dinner?" She yelled from the kitchen to the front porch where she had a good view of me. I got up from playin' with the ant that seemed lost tryin' to carry a kernel of popcorn. I opened the screen door and talked to momma. The first thing that came out of my mouth was, "some fried chicken!"

I didn't care what other beef or steak was in there, chicken was my favorite. I remember once when money was low and all momma could afford to get from the grocery store was chicken. We had baked, fried, barbequed, and broiled chicken that whole week. I thought I was gone wake up cluckin' and layin' eggs. I didn't complain though, 'cuz I was just as full as any other kid.

"I'm tired of chicken Berry. You can't think of anything else with all this food in here?" Momma seemed irritated with my cravin'. "Then, can we have some tacos?" I also loved Mexican food. Somewhere in our family tree I believe there was a person of Mexican or Latino decent. Jeremy and I both would bounce off the walls for a good taco or burrito. Then again, we bounced off the wall for anything momma cooked. She could season a brick and make it taste like steak.

Momma agreed on tacos. "Girl you betta close my screen door. You lettin' flies in here Berry. Where's Jeremy and Damon?" I responded with my nose pressed on the screen. "They went to the playground to look at some girls and told me I couldn't go. I tried to sound disappointed, but momma didn't entertain my performance. She just kept seasonin' her meat. "You don't need to be runnin' the streets with them boys! Go wash yo' hands and come help me cook." I was much obliged.

The tacos were on the table when momma and I heard Jeremy and Damon run on the porch. Damon was hidin' behind the black and gold metal rocker. Jeremy came in the house lookin' "big- eyed", as momma used to say. "What's goin' on Jeremy?" She could read any expression on our faces. Momma knew our body's better than we did. She jumped up from the dinner table and went to the door to see Damon still kneeled beside the rocker. A short light skinned man wearin' a straw hat and grey cow boy boots approached the steps. His blue and grey checked shirt coordinated perfectly.

"How-do-you-do ma'am? I'm Donald Jankins. Are the parents of the household in?" He removed his hat to reveal his sweaty, balding, salt and pepper hair. "I'm the parent of the house. How can I help you Sir?" Momma had a worried look on her face. Jeremy crept to the front door. I turned the t.v. down so I could hear what was about to be said. "Ma'am, do you have two son's that live here? I followed them for a couple of blocks from the park." Momma replied anxiously, "I have a son and a daughter. What's goin' on? Damon, come from over there! Get out here Jeremy!" Momma talked through her teeth as she commanded Jeremy and Damon to show their faces.

"These two boys was throwin' rocks at my car and one of 'em hit my tail light. He pointed at the passenger tail light of the car parked along the curb in front of our house. "I wanna know who the hell gone pay for it?" His scratchy, country voice went up an octave. "Which one of ya hit this man's car?" Jeremy and Damon looked at each other but neither responded to the question. "I'm not gone ask a second time!" Momma raised her voice. Jeremy answered quickly like he was about 6 years old, "I ain't throw that rock. Damon chimed in, "I didn't either." Momma continued to look them both in the eyes as she looked back and forth at them. I could tell she was tryin' to see who would crack first. Jeremy looked serious and stood side by side with momma. Damon was now sittin' in the rocker lookin' down at his clean Fila sneakers.

"Well, I'm sorry Mr. Jankins, but they don't seem to

know who broke yo' tail light." "That's bullshit!" Mr. Jankins walked like he wanted to come up our stairs. Jeremy moved to the top of the first stair and Damon was to the right of him. Both with their eyebrows turned down. Mr. Jankins paused put his hat back on. "Excuse me Mr. Jankins, but you will not come to my house cursin' at my kids. I understand you bein' mad about yo light, but I know when my son is lyin' to me and this is not one of the times he is. If you didn't see them throw the rock, then with all due respect sir, you don't know who threw it."

Mr. Jankins looked down at the ground like a tamed puppy. "All I'm sayin' is that I saw these boys running after they saw me get out to check my car. If they ain't guilty, then why'd they run?" Momma turned to Jeremy and Damon for the answer. "Sistah Brandy, we started runnin' because he told us if his car had a scratch on it he was gone shoot us!" Damon looked to Jeremy for solidity in his story. Before Jeremy could add anything to the story, momma interjected. With her hands on her finely curved hips, momma moved closer to the edge of the stairs. Her light brown eyes squinted as she looked Mr. Jankins in the eyes and said, "Did you tell these boys that Mr. Jankins?" She never blinked as she stood there blank faced waitin' for him to respond. Mr. Jankins looked and laughed nervously. "Now I just told 'em that to scare 'em. I wasn't gone shoot 'em." Momma just looked at him. She was still expressionless. "I hope you wasn't, 'cuz then you would have had another problem on yo' hands Sir."

"Ma'am, I apologize for that. Listen, can you please just make sure it don't happen again? All of this could have been avoided." Momma cut Mr. Jankins off. "You right! It could have been avoided if you'd just pulled them to the side and asked them instead o' threatenin' to shoot them." Mr. Jankins turned around, got in his car, and drove away. "Y'all go in the house and get ready fo' dinner. This mess don't make no sense." Even though momma was mad, she knew Jeremy and Damon weren't lyin'......so she thought. I just so happened to see Jeremy give Damon five behind momma's back. If momma were to find out, the neighbors six blocks over would hear Jeremy's screams for help. Growin' up we were always told, "You ain't too old to get yo' ass whooped!"

Just as Jeremy fought the tall weeds and smell of somethin' dead in the air while takin' the trash to the dumpster in the alley, sistah Beulah pulled up in the driveway. She blew the horn and then proceeded to walk up on the porch. "Brandy? It's me." She knocked once and turned the knob. Momma hated when people walked in her house without bein' invited. Sistah Beulah was guilty of that every time she went to a person's house. It didn't really matter though, 'cuz momma kept our storm door locked. Sistah Beulah had no choice but to wait until momma came to the door.

"Thank you Brandy. You just don't know how much you've helped me today." Momma shook her head and waved her hand. "Beulah, you know you welcome girl. It wasn't no big problem." Sistah Beulah looked confused with momma's remark. "Where's Damon? Was he a problem?" For some reason momma avoided that question. Instead she responded, "He went out the back to help Jeremy take the trash out. Is everything o.k. with Tirianna?" Momma seemed anxious to know what the situation was. Although she didn't gossip to anyone, she loved to hear the gossip. Sistah Beulah searched for words. "Girl yeah, she's fine. She out there sittin' in the car. I'm gone have to really work with that girl!" Her nervous laugh was a dead give-away that somethin' was wrong and she was too ashamed to say. She just shook her head. "I'm sure she'll be alright Beulah. Just pray and ask God for guidance sistah. He may not come when you need Him......," momma reassured sistah Beulah.

"Jeremy?" Momma realized that Jeremy and Damon hadn't come back from takin' out the garbage. "Berry go see what them two up too." For some reason I felt like momma was tryin' to get me out of the kitchen so she and sistah Beulah could further discuss Tirianna's problem. I didn't mind though, 'cuz I knew momma would end up tellin' me and Jeremy anyway; maybe not today, but someday. I walked to the back door to get Jeremy and Damon. When I went out the back and onto the porch, Jeremy and Damon were comin' out of the garage. "Jeremy? Momma want you!" Damon sistah Beulah in the house waitin' for you." Jeremy hurried toward the porch before I could come down the last stair. "Come on Berry." He completely turned me around and made me change direction. He and Damon whispered somethin' and then Damon said, "You know it! I will definitely be fallin' through so we can kick it." Jeremy agreed, "Make sure you do that."

I wasn't sure what was happenin' or what I missed, but Damon and Jeremy were actin' strange as ever. It wasn't like Jeremy to keep secrets from me, so I figured this had to be big. Nothin' I could think of had any direct relevance to the garage. Unless it was a stolen car! Oooooooooo! I remember thinkin', "Jeremy done stole somebody's car." The suspense was killing me. Guess I'm gonna have to take a little trip to the garage. I would figure the time and day out later. I knew Jeremy was on guard about the shack with the fallin' doors where we never parked our car. The way he acted confirmed that takin' a peek wouldn't be as easy as I'd expected. My planning stages would begin sometime tonight when Jeremy sneaked outta the house. He sneaked out regularly because he thought momma and I both were sleepin'. There were plenty of nights he got blamed for leavin' the t.v on all night. Of course he couldn't say anything. I dared him!

Life 101- First Day of Class

Today is September 12th, 1988. I'm over excited because tomorrow is my sixteenth birthday. The day was cloudy, but the temperature was a cool seventy degrees. The weather for the next few days was gone be pleasant too. Things had really changed around the house and in our lives. The house had been completely redone. Jeremy bought the most expensive furniture that would fit in our home. The kitchen was now decorated with a new wood finished floor and matchin' cabinets. The Whirlpool side by side refrigerator was never empty. We always had food in it and on the days we didn't, all we had to do is go to the matchin' deep freezer in the basement and get somethin' out to cook. The General Electric stove was momma's favorite. She loved the timer and the light so she could check on the progress of her baked goods without even openin' the oven door. She especially liked the smooth stove top because she only had to wipe it down after cookin'. Even though I took over the majority of cookin' responsibilities, momma still helped out and cooked whenever she was feelin' well.

Jeremy kept bringin' in bags of food and pans for the festivities tomorrow. He'd really grown into the man he always wanted to be. Dad would have been so proud of him.......somewhat. He and momma planned my party down to the tee. The menu included macaroni and cheese, fried chicken, string beans with white potatoes, meatballs and gravy, and all the crab legs a person thought they might wanna eat. Sistah Beulah was due over sometime later to help momma prepare the meat. I couldn't help because I was about to go to the mall with Jeremy's girlfriend Cassie. Cassie was the girl at the mall that gave Jeremy all the hook-ups on the latest tennis shoes. She was a nice girl too; always dressed nice when she wasn't in her work uniform and she kept her hair and nails done. She drove a clean black '87 Beretta with painted designs on it. She and Jeremy had only been together for a few months, but she was "real." Not flaky like some of the dirt bags Jeremy had caressed between the sheets. A lot of them were only nice to me because they knew I played an important part in Jeremy's life. I never liked any of them but Cassie was different. She wasn't in it for the money because she had her own and she had style and class about herself.

When I heard Cassie's horn, I ran out the door excitedly! "Hey Cass!" I called her the nickname Jeremy gave her. "What's up Berry? You ready for a day at the mall?" Cassie smiled as she grabbed her compact from her miniature Gucci purse. "You know it! Oh, wait! I forgot to get the money from Jeremy." I opened the car door to go back in the house, but Jeremy was comin' from the lot next door. He'd been waitin' for the party supply people to bring the tent, table and chairs he rented. He walked up to me and gave me a hug. "You ready for your party Berry?" He seemed drained from runnin' around all day takin' care of my party and his business. He was definitely able to multitask. "Yup! I need some money though." Jeremy looked at me with a suspicious look. Probably because he had just given me a bill fifty to take care of my manicure, pedicure and hair. I'd only spent about eighty dollars, but seventy dollars was no way near enough to take care of the outfit I was dying to get. Nevertheless, Jeremy landed two more hundred dollar bills in my hand from the bundle he had in his pocket. I gave him a kiss on the lips and a wink to let him know I was truly grateful.

"How much do you need Cass?" Jeremy walked over and leaned in the driver's window stealing a kiss when Cassie turned to answer him. "What I want is in your other pocket and it's definitely not green." Jeremy blushed and looked over at me to see if I caught on. I remained straight faced like it just blew over my head. I hated hearing Jeremy talk about sex around me. "Well, you can have that anytime you want it." Jeremy leaned in to kiss Cassie again; more passionately this time. HONK, HOOOONNNNNNKKK! I leaned over in the middle of their kiss and laid my hand on the horn. "Ummm, did y'all forget that I'm in the car?" I asked frowned up with an attitude. Just as we were pullin' outta' the driveway, Angelo pulled up in his royal blue soft top Mercedes. I waved as our eyes met in the driveway. I knew he had been lookin' at me like he was diggin' me, but I continued to play him like a brother. Don't get me wrong; he was fine as hell, but I had to play the game 'cuz I knew Angelo was a dogg type nigga. Besides, if Jeremy knew the attraction was there, I would never see Angelo around our house again. That would probably be when momma and Jeremy would kick my ass simultaneously. I wasn't ready for that. I wanted to stay their 'baby' forever. It definitely had its rewards.

During the ride to the mall Cassie and I had time to chit chat as usual. Since I'd never had a big sister, I nominated her for the role. She didn't seem to mind it one bit either. We talked about when she was young and how she was an only child. She wasn't spoiled like me though. She came from a poor family and didn't know her dad personally. Only stories of him just like me and my dad. That was one of the things we had in common. Her mom used to be a high class call girl that tricked with well-known people. Cassie's dad was a former basketball player for the New York Knicks. He played center for the team and was nominated MVP for three consecutive seasons. He and her mom met during a private party for the team when they played against the Detroit Pistons at the Pontiac Silver dome. She never really talked about how her mom got into the 'escort' business, but she did say her mom was top of the line; including her prices. Yup, a high price hoe. (That was how *she* put it!) When her dad found out a child was conceived from their two month fling, he'd behest her to get rid of it.

Cassie said her mom told her that of all the tricks she'd had, she's never ended up pregnant and that to her, this must have been some type of sign from God to change her life. When she refused to terminate the pregnancy, Cassie's dad was infuriated and tried to have Cassie's mom killed. His attempts were unsuccessful and Cassie's mom never ended up pressin' charges nor did she reveal the name of her child's father. Only Cassie and her mom knew who he was. She had pictures of him and her mom at various events though. Seems he often requested Cassie's mom's services. Anyhow, Cassie's mom had a nervous breakdown while trying to raise her by herself. She'd exhausted all of her earnings by the time Cassie was sixteen. She just couldn't take being poor again. Eventually she ended up on heroin and tried to commit suicide. Now she's in a mental institution. Cassie still visits her regularly though, but her mom never acknowledges her presence. She's considered class A, incoherent and suicidal at the mental hospital so all of her visits are supervised. Cassie spoke about it like she'd been tellin' the story all her life. All I could do was imagine how she must have felt as a child carryin' all that hurt. I thought to myself, "Damn! Cassie is so strong."

"So kiddo, are you having sex yet?" I was taken aback. I really didn't know how to answer that question because not only is Cassie Jeremy's girlfriend; she was also a stranger to me no matter how "cool" she was. Sure, she and Jeremy dated for a couple of months, but was I really ready to disclose classified information to her? "What made you ask me that?" I asked nervously and suspiciously. Was Cassie a spy for Jeremy? "No offense Berry, I just thought that we could talk about it. I didn't mean to pry." I glanced over at her while she drove lookin' straight ahead. I wanted to see if she was bein' "real" or if she was just tryin' to be up in my business.

I don't know what made me put up my guard, because actually I hadn't been sexually active yet. The boys in my school were a no-no. Jeremy always taught me that, "a broke nigga ain't got shit to offer but a bunch of promises that were destined to be broken." There were some that wanted to hook up but I just wasn't interested. I was the best dressed female in school and I had an image to uphold. I never acted snoody or looked down on people though. Momma taught me that I should be thankful of everything I had no matter what the situation was; those were the words I lived by. I didn't have female friends because they just weren't 'my thing'. I didn't have time for gossip and he-say-she-say and I really could care less about another person's problems.

Besides, the majority of them only wanted to hang out with me because they wanted Jeremy. What's funny is that they thought I wasn't smart enough to figure it out. With the current events in our household I would never jeopardize my brother and his extra-curricular activities. My home was my safe haven and that's exactly how I wanted to keep it.

"No offense taken Cassie. I'm just trippin' 'cuz you know how females are." I laughed to downplay my insecurity. "Naw, I haven't had sex yet. But I can't say I don't think about it……more often than not." Cassie laughed to herself. "I know what you mean!" I was hopin' I wouldn't have to reach over and punch her lights out because for some reason I felt a "Jeremy" story comin' on. I frowned. Cassie continued the conversation as we merged onto the Jeffries freeway headed towards Fairlane Mall in Dearborn. "Berry, there's nothing wrong with thinkin' about sex. Sex is a beautiful thing at times. And yes, it does feel good when it's shared between two people that have feelings for one another." Her voice was light and soothing. She made me feel at ease enough to start askin' the questions that I was afraid to ask momma and petrified to bring up with Jeremy. "How old were you when you had sex Cassie?" I waited anxiously for her response. Although my question seemed to irritate her, she answered quick and sharp like she anticipated what I was goin' to say next. "My situation was different Berry. My mother was on drugs by the time I turned sixteen and we were poor as dirt." We didn't have anyone to turn to." I was wonderin' where her story was goin' and what that had to do with my question to her. I sat there lookin' puzzled. "To answer your question, I was thirteen when I started having sex." Her answer shocked me. I couldn't imagine being thirteen and havin' sex! Hell, at the age of thirteen I was still playing jax and carryin' around the Cabbage Patch doll that my grandmother bought me for gettin' good grades. My next inquiry was, "is it really a difference between makin' love and havin' sex?"

There was a long pause before Cassie continued. I sat there thinkin' about what all I was doin' when I turned thirteen. I was attracted to boys at that age though. I probably would have dropped my panties for Myron if he'd sneezed too hard! He was too damn fine. But I don't even think he was into sex at that time. "I didn't even *like* the person I slept with for the first time", Cassie continued. I gave my virginity to a complete stranger!" Cassie looked as if she was disgusted with the thought. I sat quietly not knowin' what was goin' through her mind. "Listen Berry, the difference between sex and love making all depends on the person. Love making should be with the person you care about. Feelings are involved and you get goose bumps when you talk to that person or when that person comes around; kind of like Jeremy and I." I balled my right fist preparin' for her to go into detail about my brother. I was gone sock her right in her left temple. She continued on with her theory. "Sex is something that should be done for a reason; survival, monetary purposes." Cassie had my undivided attention. Besides the things I'd heard females in the school lavatory talk about and stuff I'd seen on TV, I was really unknowledgeable about sex. I thought for the longest that I could get pregnant without even havin' my period. Momma did correct me on that though.

"See Berry, a lot of guys out here just want to fuck with

no strings attached!" Her words blew my mind. In the short time I'd known Cassie I'd never heard her speak so bluntly before. "Sure, they'll tell you they love you and want you in their lives and all of that crap, but really all they want to do is get into your panties, sample the goods, and call it a day." Cassie merged into the right lane to come up on Ford Road. "For those types, you make 'em pay." I looked over at her sharp with one eyebrow up. "Why are you looking at me like that?" Her long lashes blinked rapidly as she glanced over at me. "So, are you tellin' me it's o.k. to get paid for doin' *it?*" My thoughts started to race. Is this bitch crazy? Is Jeremy payin' her? I thought I should jump out and catch a cab home, but that thought quickly left my mind. I had to get this outfit for my birthday. But as soon as I got it I was catchin' a cab back to the crib. As we entered the parkin' lot racin' for a close spot, Cassie said, "If you're going to let him hit your 'spot', then why not tap off into his knot? Nothing is free in this world Berry; Nothing!" Cassie was as serious as a lump in a woman's breast. I heard her and I truly understood what she was sayin'. I appreciated her honesty and the fact that she was even schoolin' me on the ways of the world. I would definitely take this conversation into consideration......when the time comes. Right now, I'm dying to find my killer birthday gear that would complement my killer birthday body! Later for sex talk! At this very moment the mall stores are callin' my name.

Back at the house, Jeremy continued to scramble around tryin' to get everything together for the party. Angelo parked in the driveway and Jeremy went to greet him. "What's up? Jeremy smiled and slapped hands with Angelo as he climbed out of the car. His Timberland boots complimented his green Guess jeans and jacket. His silver name plated belt buckle shined like new money. It read: Lo-Down! The perfect words to describe his thuggish demeanor.

Angelo had sexed up a few females around the neighborhood and his list included Dorrie, Mrs. Sherry's granddaughter. She would visit a lot on the weekends when we were younger, but Mrs. Sherry never let her play or socialize with anyone from our neighborhood. Her granddaughter was too "good" for us. I remember when Dorrie would catch the bus to Mrs. Sherry's house after school. She would walk past our house and not even speak. Jeremy said he tried to holler at her when they were teenagers and she would look at him like he was beneath her; until he started gettin' money that is. Once she saw how many niggaz would be over our house in various cars, she started grinnin' at Jeremy and walkin' with her ass tooted out. Jeremy wouldn't give her the time of day though.

Anyway, she started messin' around with Angelo; what did she do that for? He started off bein' nice to her, but once he realized how much of a snobbish bitch she really was, he started treatin' her like she deserved to be treated. Like the shit she *thought* she was all along. One summer she called herself frontin' him around Jeremy and a couple of other regulars at our house. I guess Mrs. Sherry's old ass told her that he was at our house after he canceled a date with her. How dare him cancel on her! She walked next door to our driveway and asked Angelo, "Can I speak with you?" Of course Angelo put on a front for his fella's, "I'm busy." He continued smokin' his cigarette and conversin' with the male assembly in front of the driveway. "NOW De Angelo!" She said his full first name and talked firm like she had him in check. Angelo stopped talkin' to the cluster of guys standin' around and just looked at her. "Man, leave that hoe alone dog! She ain't even worth it." One guy must have known what was about to happen next. He tried to take Angelo's attention off of Dorrie's distasteful behavior.

When Angelo ignored her continued his meaningless conversation about how much money he'd won shootin' dice three nights prior, Dorrie walked over to him and grabbed him by his silk shirt. SMAACK! Just that quick. Dorrie fell straight on her flat ass! Everybody on the block was crackin' up. Jeremy helped her up off the ground and told her to go home. He got on Angelo too for disrespectin' our house by puttin' his hands on a girl. Angelo apologized to Jeremy but he didn't say shit to Dorrie.

That's when Mrs. Sherry brought her evil ass down there tryin' to talk to momma about what happened. Momma told her, "I ain't got nothin' to do with what that young man did; he ain't my child." Mrs. Sherry tried to make light of the situation by smilin' and suggestin' maybe momma shouldn't have him around anymore. She told momma she didn't want to have to shoot him if he put his hands on her grandchild again. That's when Jeremy butted in, "As long as you don't shoot him in front of our house!" Mrs. Sherry was livid! The wrinkles in her face increased rapidly as she scowled. She just walked off the porch and went back next door. That's around the time momma had to check out on Mrs. Sherry.

"I was just comin' from over the way to check on my spot." Angelo explained to Jeremy as if he had to have a reason for stopping by. "You got everything you need or is it time to restock?" Jeremy leaned on the side of the privacy fence as the party suppliers pulled up in front of the house. "Tell them to come to the side Jeremy!" Momma yelled from the front porch. She came to the door when she noticed the white four door van pull up in front of the house. Angelo and Jeremy moved to the side as the crew hauled in the tent, tables and chairs for tomorrow's "holiday."

"As a matter of fact I got some new shit in that I need you to put out there." Jeremy continued his conversation with Angelo as they headed towards the garage. Momma was outside directin' traffic. "O.k. we want the tent over here and this space should be left clear for the D.J. booth...." Momma looked cute in her little Nike nylon joggin' suit that Jeremy and I got her for her last birthday. It was pink and blue and her pulled back ponytail made her look like she was our older sister. "Hey Mrs. McDaniel." Angelo spoke to momma as he bent down to kiss her cheek. "You need help with anything?" He was grinnin' from ear to ear. A lot of Jeremy's friend's had a crush on momma. They would tease Jeremy about how "fine" momma was; especially when they would see her dressed up on Sunday's. "I'm fine baby. Jeremy? When is the D.J. comin' to set up?" Jeremy looked surprised. "Dang! I forgot to get a D.J.!" Momma yelled, "What we gone do about music?" Angelo quickly interjected, "I can get a D.J. for y'all. My cousin owes me a favor.....a few actually. I'll call him tonight." Momma looked disappointed. "You think you can get him on such short notice?" "Don't worry Mrs. McDaniel. If I can't get him I'll come over and D.J. myself!" Jeremy and Angelo assured momma that everything would work out as they headed towards the garage. "Ma, pay the crew and I'll give it back to you." Jeremy spoke to momma as he fumbled with the lock on the garage door.

After momma supervised the party supply crew, she had to sign off on a contract sayin' that she received everything she ordered and make a payment. As she turned to go in the house and get the money, Sistah Beulah came out to observe the newly decorated vacant lot. "Ooh Brandy! This is beautiful!" Her eyes were as big as silver dollars. The round tables were placed three feet apart and seated six people to a table. There were ten tables. The D.J.'s table was closest to the garage so that he could use the electrical outlets from the garage. The food tables were off to the side so the entrées could be brought out from the back door easily. There was another round table to the left that had a light blue skirt around it unlike the food and D.J. table dressed with white skirts. There was an area in the yard left open closer to the front. That's where Jeremy had one of the local fiend's to build him a stage that stood about four inches off the ground. It was wide enough for at least twenty people to dance at once. It was covered with green outdoor carpeting like what we had on our porch.

Sistah Beulah continued to look around in amazement. Before, it was just an empty lot that we'd placed a privacy fence around. Sure, we had a table with an umbrella and chairs, but this was like a really sophisticated look. "Once I put those table cloths and candles on, it's gone add the finishin' touch." Momma agreed as she went to get the money to pay for the set up. "Now all you need is some lights along the fence." Sistah Beulah made the suggestion as momma's back disappeared through the back door.

"Now that's a good idea!" Angelo chimed in as he walked briskly through the yard to his car. He was carrying a K-mart bag that sagged like it was heavy. "Aw'ight Jeremy! I'll be back man. I gotta go try to hook up wit' this cat so I can bring him to set up. I'll bring Berry's gift when I come back too." Jeremy responded, "Don't be bullin' man. We need a D.J. so I won't have momma comin' down on my head". Jeremy was careful not to curse while Sistah Beulah sat at the table still lookin' around. "I got you man!" Angelo reassured Jeremy that he would come through as he closed the trunk on his Mercedes. "I'll see you in a minute." Angelo whipped in reverse and headed down McKinley.

"Excuse me sir." Jeremy turned to see one of the set up people waitin' in the driveway. He didn't pay attention as he and Angelo walked right past him. "I'm waiting to be paid. The lady said she would be back with the money but I've been standing here for about fifteen minutes." Jeremy shouted towards the back door. "Ma?" He thought momma was in the kitchen preparing something. Sistah Beulah chimed in, "I'll get her Jeremy. I gotta go and get the candles and table clothes anyway." Sistah Beulah's pleated red skirt shifted from side to side as she waltzed her full sized hips up the stairs. Just as she entered the kitchen, momma stood starin' towards the livin' room lookin' flustered. She was fillin' around her bosom and checkin' her pockets. "Brandy, the people out there waitin' for you to pay 'em." Momma kept focusin' on the livin' room floor. "What 'cha done lost?" Sistah Beulah followed suit lookin' down at the floor.

"I know I had it before I went outside with them tent people." Momma became frantic. "Beulah, look under the kitchen table and see if you see my purple pocketbook.

Sistah Beulah obliged at momma's request. "Ain't nothin' under this table Brandy; not even a crumb! Girl, I shole wish you was still cleanin' houses. You can find all kinds of mess under my kitchen table." Sistah Beulah chuckled but momma didn't respond. She was over by the side of stove lookin' on the floor. "Ma? Did you get the money to pay these people?" Jeremy pressed his clean shaven face against the screen on the back storm door. "I can't find my pocketbook Jeremy. I think I might of dropped it out there when they came to set up." Momma looked wearily over at Jeremy hopin' that her lost pocketbook hadn't been discovered by one of the many visitors that stopped by that day.

"Hold on a second man!" Jeremy came in and ran upstairs to his stash in the bedroom. Nobody knew about Jeremy's suitcase in the closet but me and him. He told me about it just in case we ever fell behind in the bills again or if he ever went to jail and needed to post bail. He didn't tell momma because he felt like the less she knew about his pharmaceutical business, the better off she was. Nevertheless, he didn't play on her intelligence. He kept everything outside in the garage so momma wouldn't have to be embarrassed by the police if they ended up raiding the house.

Jeremy came down the stairs countin' out the money for the party set up. He bumped into sistah Beulah as she stood organizin' the cooked food on the counter. Just as she moved the meatballs over to the side to grab the aluminum foil, she screamed. "Here it is Brandy! Here go that pocketbook you was lookin' for." She held the tattered imitation leather purse in the air so momma could see it as she lifted her hand from

D'Aviér

her head. "God is good!" Momma sighed with relief as sistah Beulah tossed it to her. "Now maybe this damn headache will disappear."

" Well, I'm about to go put these ribs on the grill Brandy. Can you get the door for me?" Momma walked over and held the door open for sistah Beulah. "You need help with that?" Jeremy was back at the back door tryin' to grab the metal pan from sistah Beulah. "I got it Jeremy, but you can pass me the seasoned water on the counter just in case a fire starts in the grill." Jeremy walked up and kissed momma on the cheek as she stood at the sink takin' medication to ease the pain in her temples. "I got my pocketbook! Sistah Beulah found it on the counter next to the meatballs." Jeremy looked towards the spot momma pointed to. "It's too late now ma; I already paid them. I gave the guy a couple of extra dollars for his patience. Did you put it up where you could find it?" She pulled it out of her bosom to show Jeremy.

"Jeremy, pass me the cheese out the refrigerator." Momma walked over to the stove to turn off the macaroni noodles she had boiling. "You need me to grate it for you ma? Everything else is done." Momma raced the hot pot over to the sink to drain the noodles. "If you not expectin' anybody to come over." She spoke with sarcasm in her voice.

Heiress Heirloom

Jeremy sat at the kitchen table and began to open the thick block of Focus Hope government cheese. "You know Jeremy, your father used to be in them streets too. I never told you this, but that's how I met your dad." Jeremy sat quietly as he continued to help momma. He and momma rarely had heart to heart conversations like she and I. Jeremy was always too busy tryin' to provide for and protect us. Whenever they did communicate, it was usually between Jeremy comin' and goin' from the house to the garage. He was always home, but never in the house for a long period of time. He never really got settled until after three or four in the mornin'. He would even be up and dressed by nine in the mornin'.

Momma continued with her story. "Your father hung out with all the gang bangers in the hood. He didn't have beef with anybody and they all respected him. It didn't matter who he knew or socialized with from what area or gang, they all kicked it with him and respected the fact that he was neutral. Never once did Jeremy let the streets compromise his decision to *stay* neutral either. I see a lot of him in you. I just don't want you to get hurt Jeremy. The streets today ain't nothin' like they was when your dad and I was comin' up; they much worse now." Jeremy looked up at momma as he continued to grate the cheese and his knuckles. "Awww, ma! What you talkin' about? Ain't nothin' gone happen to me."

She continued to talk as if she knew what Jeremy's next

response would be. "I was born at night Jeremy but not last night, ok? Don't think for one minute I don't know what's goin' on in or around my own house!" Momma began to get irritated. Talkin' to Jeremy was one thing, but gettin' him to really listen was another. Momma washed her hands after she laid the first layers of noodles and mild cheddar cheese in the bottom of the extra-large aluminum pan. After she dried her hands she pulled the tattered purple pocketbook from her bosom.

"I think it's about time for you to hear the story behind this pocketbook Jeremy." Momma tossed the pocketbook in front of Jeremy as she pulled a chair back front the kitchen table. She sat right next to Jeremy so she could have direct eye contact. We knew momma was serious when she looked us in our eyes. She always told us that our eyes were the direct path to our souls and when she would speak serious, she was lookin' in our souls and she wanted us to do the same to hers.

She proceeded with the story.............

Heiress gave me this pocket book back when I was Berry's age. She was my best friend when I lived with your grandparents. We met each other in third grade on our way to Custer Elementary over on Linwood. Heiress lived two houses over in a two-family flat with her mother and grandmother. She was tall and thin with a big butt for her small frame. She and I were the same complexion and both wore our hair in two French braids at that time. Our eyes were even the same color! We did everything together. If I wasn't at her house, she was at mines. People in the hood actually thought we was cousins. Her grandmother, Ms. Burton, said she named her Heiress because if anything were to happen to her, Heiress would inherit her 'estate'. A black Delta Eighty-Eight and the fortune she saved from being a school crossing guard twenty years earlier. That was all they had besides the brick two family flat that was sure to be hers for the takin'. Heiress had everything a girl could want. Her mother told us how when she got pregnant with Heiress, Ms. Burton refused to spend another hard earned dime on her. So instead, her money went towards takin' care of Heiress. As if she needed anything else. She was rotten to the core! I didn't do too bad myself. But anything I didn't have could be found in Heiresses' bedroom. The two of us were inseparable from the day we met until the day she died.

Momma had Jeremy's undivided attention. He'd finished shreddin' the cheese and took a wet napkin to soothe his scraped knuckles. She spoke slowly and very clearly as if there was about to be some type of message she was attemptin' to relay to him. Sistah Beulah walked in to make more water for the barbeque. The fire was just right at this point. Momma never looked up nor acknowledged sistah Beulah. She made more of the vinegar and water solution and left back out the back door; tryin' not to be her usual nosey self. Either that, or she knew she needed to handle her own situations at home.

One evening, after I went home and did my chores and homework, I walked over to Heiresses' so we could talk junk and act silly like we usually did when we were together. After we finished listenin' to our Chaka Khan and Rufus greatest hits, Heiress wanted to walk up to the gas station on Fenkell and Doris, about three blocks down from her house on the other side of Linwood. I knew she just wanted to go up there and meet "Papa". He was a well-known banger from 12th Street. All Heiress talked to were bangers; high profile bangers at that. Leaders of gangs were her specialty. They kept her donned in the latest fashions and name brands. It got to the point where her bi-weekly hundred and fifty dollar wardrobe allowance became her every day pocket money. She had all of the boys' attention when we would go skatin' at the roller rink in Southfield. She loved it and so did I! Every guy she socialized with had a friend just for me.

"Papa" was bad news from the start, but you couldn't tell Heiress that. Her nose was wide open for "Papa". I couldn't see why 'cuz he wasn't even a touch of cute! He was black as night with pink lips and a missin' tooth in the front. Rumor has it that before he started bangin' he was just an average neighborhood punk that got bullied by the bigger boys around the hood. It was said that his tooth was knocked out 'cuz he finally tried to stand up for hisself. He eventually started workin' out and hangin' with some of the locals who felt sorry for him. I guess he worked his way up through the ranks. At that point he was a mass of muscles and biceps, terrifyin' people in the area by pistol whippin' folk and hittin' people in the knees with bats and shit. It was just a matter of time before somebody got his ass back.

Heiress knew I wasn't really feelin' "Papa". I never told her, but there were a few occasions where I saw him ridin' with other females in his car. She was delighted by the sight of his sorry butt and I just didn't want to be the one to ruin that feelin' for her. "Come on Brandy!" Heiress was doin' that whinin' stuff that she knew irritated me. I gave her a look that could sink a cruise line. My left eyebrow was turned up and I clinched my teeth like I always did to let her know how irritated I really was with her child-like antics of tryin' to persuade me to go with her. She just had a way of convincin' me to do whatever she wanted. She always won in the long run. I guess her charm was her gift. That's what made so many guys come out of pocket like they did; her charm along with some other thangs!

"Alright! Heiress, dang! But you betta go get me a knife out the kitchen. I ain't walkin' across Fenkell unarmed!" Heiress frowned at my request. "Girl, you been over here all your life. You know damn near everybody over here, besides the renters." I didn't return a reply to her sarcasm. That's how Heiress knew when I was serious. I wouldn't budge nor reply once I put my foot down about somethin'; yo' daddy realized it too as time went on in our courtin' days.

Heiress took her butt in the house and got me a knife like I asked. She knew if she didn't there would be no sneakin' to see "Papa's" tired ass that night. Just as Heiress rolled her eyes at me and closed the storm door, her phone rang. She picked it up on the second ring tryin' not to draw attention to her attempts to see Papa. Her grandmother wasn't aware of Heiress's boyfriend's extra-curricular activities. She'd never met Papa because his reputation preceded him around the hood. When Ms. Burton would hear one of the other neighbors talk about him she would always say, " If I ever catch his long armed ass around here doin' something' to somebody, I'mma put a cap in his ass! He betta' stay his ass away from 'round here!." Ms. Burton had a way about herself that let people know she wasn't one to be mistreated.   Maybe it was the one incident that happened about twelve years ago. She laid some young guy out right in her front yard. He broke into her house and she caught him with one leg in the window and one leg out. She shot him right in the left side of his ass! When the police came he was layin' on her grass with her purse still in his hand.   He could've gotten up and ran except Ms. Burton was standin' over him with her pistol cocked until the police arrived. Hell, the police almost arrested her because they told her to drop the gun and she refused to. She started yellin' and kickin' the guy in his side.

Anyway, Heiress came out and announced it was Papa on the phone attemptin' to solidify his rendezvous with her as she passed me the butter knife wrapped in a napkin. I grabbed it and unwrapped it.   The look on my face must have told Heiress what my next statement would be. "Well, you said a knife!" I sarcastically responded, "What am I supposed to do with this Heiress? Pull it and then threatin' to smear butter all over somebody if they approach us?" We both burst into laughter. I put the knife in the back of my semi-tight Levi jeans and we started walkin'.

"That was Papa on the phone." Heiress was all too excited about seein' her "man". They'd been kickin' it for about 2 months and I guess he had her nose open. "He said he would give us a ride back home. That way you won't have to stab nobody!" Heiress was crackin' up. Her A-symmetric haircut swung softly over her little perfect nose.   I have to admit, I did chuckle a little to myself but little did she know, I wasn't NOT tryin' to ride in Papa's car. Hell, I didn't even want to be walkin' nowhere to meet him. But Heiress needed me to go. After all, that's what friends are for.

Once we got past the boys home and started approaching the gas station, I spotted Papa's gray Lincoln Continental. He was parked beside the phone booth with the lights out. It was as if he was being extra careful to remain incognito. When we stepped past the hospital launder company, Heiress was in full view of the discreet vehicle. "There he is Brandy! Heiress started trottin' towards Papa's car. He cut the headlights on in acknowledgement of her smile and waves. The car was now idled and pullin' up to the far left hand pump that sat around five feet from the entrance. Heiress met Papa with a kiss as she leaned into the driver side window.

"I'll be out in a minute Heiress!" I spoke loud as I walked past the car. I wanted to let her know that her visit wouldn't be as long as she'd probably anticipated. "How you doin' Ms.Brandy?" Papa sounded like he was tryin' to sound sexy when he spoke. His raspy voice was like long fingernails goin' down a chalkboard. My face immediately disfigured. I started not to speak to his sneaky ass, but I was always raised that it won't kill you to part your lips and speak to a person. Besides, my back was facing him. I spoke to him with that shitty look on my face. He didn't notice a difference because whenever he spoke, I would always reply dryly.

The gas station seemed unusually empty tonight for some reason. Maybe it was because of the Tina Marie & Rick James concert down at the Masonic Temple in Downtown Detroit. I'd heard a few people around the neighborhood say that they were goin' to check it out. On any given night the gas station would be frequented by high school kids hangin' out right on the corner of Doris; just kickin' it and talkin' mess. The majority of the time the bangers would meet up before makin' a surprise visit to stomp a hole in somebody's butt. That was before it was so easy to get a hold of a "piece."

The walk from Linwood and the Lodge service drive made me thirsty. I decided to get me a Faygo Rock-n-Rye soda and a couple of bags of punkin' seeds. I loved punkin' seeds; the kind that came in the red bag with the Indian on the front. When I got to the counter to pay, I realized that I'd left my money in my jacket pocket back at Heiress's house. I only had on my Gloria Vanderbilt shirt that was just as tight as my jeans, because Heiress was sneakin' out and I didn't have a chance to grab my jacket. I'd left a *few* clothin' items at her house that way; helpin' her sneak out and then goin' home afterwards. It wasn't a problem though 'cuz we stayed in each other's clothes.

I was a dollar short of the dollar fifty I owed for my purchase, so I told the Arab cashier to hang on while I hollered out the door to Heiress. He was skeptical at first, but after he talked trash under his breath he finally agreed to let me take the two steps to the door to get it from Heiress. Just as I pushed the door open to get Heiress's attention, I noticed that I hit this guy comin' in the gas station with the steel handle on the door. "Oops! I am so sorry! Are you alright?" I was apologetic and concerned. He moved his hand from his side like he was checkin' to see if he was bleedin'. "I'm alright love." Once he looked into my eyes I was taken aback. His deep voice and glossy chocolate skin was so appealing to me. "Are you alright?" He returned the concern. "I'm fine. I didn't mean to…..." He stopped me in mid-sentence. "There's no need for apologies. Were you about to leave? Here, let me get the door for you." All I could do was stare at him. I just kept thinkin' about Diana Ross in *Lady Sings the Blues*, when Billy Dee Williams asked her, "You want my arm to fall off?" I told him that I just wanted to holler out the door to my friend.

"By all means!" He extended his soft lookin' smooth hand as if he were givin' me permission to leave out the door. I was kind of nervous to walk past him; wasn't sure if I could contain myself! Plus, I just knew he would be lookin' at my butt! I had them child bearin' hips goin' on back then.

As I peeked out of the bullet proof glass door, I shouted to Heiress to let me borrow the change I needed. Unbeknownst to me, the gentleman was now standin' there holdin' the door as Heiress turned around and acknowledged my request. "That's all you wanted to say to your friend?" He was bein' nosey as hell and straightforward at the same time. I turned to him like I was irritated by his meddling. He read my false facial expression. "I'm sorry to butt in but I think I may be able to help you with that! He was bein' sarcastic as he pulled out a stack of money and tossed a ten dollar bill into the medal change dish.

"You came out here hollerin' for a dollar?" Heiress had finally pried her little skinny self out of Papa's driver window. She walked up with her pocketbook in her hand. I guess she needed a break from leanin' in kissin' Papa through the window. He looked like a buffed up Pee Wee Herman with a little head that didn't really fit his body. He kept his hair done though. His pump waves were always nice and tidy; not a hair out of place. I guess he dressed nice and kept his waves neat because he didn't stand a chance with the females if he wasn't groomed; regardless to whether he had money or not. But then again, females in the neighborhood would've still kicked it with his ugly ass just because of his bad boy reputation.

"Girl! Ain't Jeremy fine?" Heiress was standin' at the front door grinnin' and whisperin' in my ear. "Who is Jeremy?" I was dumbfounded and clueless as to who she was talkin' about. "The guy that just paid for your stuff." I turned and peered at the glass door tryin' to sneak another peek after I left out the gas station. He was truly a sight for sore eyes. "How do you know him?" I wanted to be sure that this was not someone my best friend had an interest in. We never did go behind one another. Heiress explained to me that Jeremy was from around the neighborhood across Oakman. He knew the majority of bangers but never had any interest in the lifestyle. She'd told me that Papa and a couple of her previous love interests had told her bits and pieces about him, but they spoke of him with the utmost respect. He was like that character Shaft around the area. "Don't tell me you ain't gone holla at that nigga! Heiress was standin' there waitin' for a response. Her right eyebrow turned up like she was waitin' for me to say something' smart. "Girl, he only paid for my stuff 'cuz it took you too long to come in here and I was holdin' up the line! He don't even know my name Heiress. Gone back over there with Great Ape 'cuz when I come back out I'm ready to go."

"Whatever!" Heiress rolled her eyes and twisted her neck as she turned to walk back in Papa's direction. I went to the counter to grab my soda and pumpkin seeds that still sat on the counter. Just as the door closed behind me, Jeremy was walkin' back to the counter to pay for the can of 10W 40 and water he had in his hand. "So you decided to come back and give me your number hunh?" He was shufflin' through the stack of tens and ones he pulled out of his loose fitted Levis. He never even looked up at me as he spoke. I have to admit, I was flattered. My heart was racing like I'd just ran from a wild dog in the parkin' lot.

"Excuse me?" I tried to act like I didn't hear what he said. I didn't want to seem too anxious or offbeat. "Hey man?" He yelled to the gas attendant. "Let me get a pen!" He was so straight forward. The clerk put the pen inside the change dish. "So? What's your name?" He stood in front of me lookin' directly into my eyes. I was like butter as I tried to play semi-interested. I batted my eyes slowly tryin' to look as sexy as possible. "Brandy." I responded in the softest tone. "That's my favorite drink!" He replied. I was just waitin' for him to ask if he could get a taste or something corny like that. I was gone check out on his fine ass. "My name is Jeremy. Do you stay around here?" I told him that I stayed across Fenkell not far from Linwood. I was apprehensive about lettin' men know *exactly* where I stayed, just in case they thought they would be in the neighborhood and took it upon themselves to just to *drop by* one day.

Momma started to smile as she reminisced on all the fun she'd had with Heiress. She wasn't ecstatic about going to meet Papa at the gas station that night, but she realized that if it weren't for Heiress, the next chapter in her life would not have come into play. She's never trusted any females into her personal life the way she trusted Heiress; not in her adolescence nor her adult hood. Her eyes started to well up and her soft spoken voice began to crack as she searched her recollection about the night of Heiresses' death. Ironically, she'd lost the love of a companion and gained the love of another within a matter of minutes. This was the same night she fell head over heels for the man we would eventually know as our 'dad'. If only she'd been spared the heart ache of losin' them both so tragically over the years. She continued with the story as Jeremy wiped her eyes and consoled her. She finished tellin' him how daddy stole her heart and how a stranger stole the heart of Heiress in an unsuccessful attempt to seek vengeance on the person that wronged him. Momma regained her composure and continued.......

Jeremy smiled the whole time we exchanged vital information. He never stopped lookin' into my eyes. His rust colored Izod shirt showed the outline of what seemed to be a broad chest. I couldn't quite tell how built he really was because his shirt was loose fittin' like the jeans he wore. Plus the windbreaker he wore aided his attempt to camouflage his frame. Just as we were about to exit the gas station, I noticed a little boy come in with run over tennis shoes and dirty clothes. This was usually typical in the hood, but for some reason he didn't go unnoticed by me nor Jeremy.

"You got fiddy cent sir so I can buy me a juice?" Jeremy and I gave each other eye contact. I guess we both were thrown for a loop to see this barely eight years old baby out at this time of night; jacketless, and beggin' for change. All I wanted to know was where his momma was at. Just as Jeremy reached into his jacket pocket to give the boy a five dollar bill, shots were fired.

Boom! Boom! Boom! Jeremy pushed me and the little boy back from the door and onto to the dirty floor; layin' on top of us coverin' our heads. It seemed like we were layin' there forever, but it had actually only been about two or three minutes. Once the shots stopped, Jeremy rushed to his feet to check on the gas station attendant who was layin' behind the counter with his sawed off rifle. That's when I noticed Jeremy pull out a Smith and Wesson .38 special from the side of his pants before he went into the parkin' lot. I suppose this was the reason for his ill-fittin' apparel. When I saw him walk out the door, that's when it hit me! "HEIRESS!" I shouted as I jumped to my feet leavin' the minor child behind. Just as I reached the door, Jeremy pushed me back inside and yelled to the clerk, "Man, call 911!" It was then that I realized something traumatic happened and Heiress may have been involved. "Is it Heiress?" I questioned Jeremy waitin' for him to respond, but he just had this expressionless look on his face. The tears started to form in my eyes. "Answer me Jeremy! Is Heiress ok?" Still no response from Jeremy. I guess he just didn't know what to say or know how to respond.

The gas station clerk had slipped out the exit from behind the counter and was now returning. The look on his face was horrific. He picked up the phone and began speakin' in his native tongue. I couldn't understand what he was sayin' until he said in English, "Hurry up man, she's lying in the parking lot." My stomach began to knot up and a feelin' of sickness swept through. Heiress! I shouted at the top of my lungs and broke through Jeremy's grip. As I walked out I saw Papa's car, still parked in the same spot. Papa was out of the car knelt down behind the first pump. As I got closer, I could see the bullet holes in his driver side door. There was blood splattered on the door. "Oh my God! Please no! NOOOOOOO!" I ran closer, and there she was.

Papa was holdin' her, cryin' as he rocked back and forth tryin' to hold back his tears and fear. I bent down beside him and tried to grab Heiresses limp body from him. We both cried as we held her in our arms. Her eyes were closed and she had a hole about the size of a cantaloupe in her chest. She lay there lifeless, still holdin' the pocketbook in her hand from when I asked her for the change to get my stuff. I grabbed the pocketbook from her hand and stuffed it in my bra. I knew her grandmother would want it as a keepsake.

The police arrived within a few minutes and closed off the gas station. The news must have spread fast because people were everywhere. I heard Papa tell the police that he was sittin' in his car and Heiress was leanin' on his door talkin' to him, when a dark male in a blue Ford Mustang pulled up on the other side of the pump he and Heiress sat in front of. He said that he noticed the guy lookin' around suspiciously, but he didn't think anything of it because the man was pumpin' gas. What he didn't pay attention to was that this "man" never did go *into* the gas station to pay for his gas; so that was the play off. Just as Papa told Heiress to move from the door and get into the car, the man started firing. Heiress never saw it comin'. She died from the first shot. Papa laid down across the passenger seat, so he was only hit in the legs by the buck shots that came from Heiress. I lost my best friend because of Papa. He'd done so much dirt around the neighborhood and it finally caught up with him; only it was Heiress that was punished.

Jeremy had called momma and daddy to come and get me. When I finished givin' my statement to the police, I saw

Jeremy tellin' mama and daddy what happened. He'd won them over from that point on. He went with me and my parents to let Heiresses' grandmother know what happened. She ended up havin' a stroke right then and there. She couldn't bare the pain of losin' Heiress. As the ambulance wheeled her to the hospital, I gave her mother the pocketbook. "I don't want it Brandy." She fought to maintain her composure. The tears flowed rapidly down her cheeks as I hugged her and shared her grief. "You keep it. I know how close the two of you were. She would have wanted you to have it."

I've had this pocketbook since that very day. I kept a few albums that she and I exchanged. I gave the clothes that I had of hers back to her mother. I didn't want the ones I'd loaned her. But the pocketbook is my last memory of her. That's why I hold it close and panic when I misplace it.

Jeremy had tears rollin' down his cheeks. He grabbed momma and hugged her tight. "I'll be alright momma. I ain't out here doin' dirt to people like that cat Papa. Whatever happened to him anyway?" Jeremy's curiosity was aroused as he waited anxiously to hear Papa's fate. "The police found his naked body over by the railroad tracks behind the old bakery off Oakman about a month after Heiress was killed. His hands were tied behind his back and his tongue was missin'. Somebody beat him to death and cut his tongue out. Neither his killer nor Heiresses' killer was ever caught. Some people around the hood said the little boy that was in the gas station that night witnessed Papa beat his father up about steppin' on his white tennis shoes. The theory is that the little boy was sent in the gas station to keep us preoccupied so we wouldn't come out of the store. We never did see him again after that." "Momma grabbed Jeremy's hand that was twice the size of hers and looked into her brown eyes. "Jeremy, I know you ain't makin' an earnest livin' around here. I just don't say nothin' because I know you doin' yo' best to look out for me and Berry. I just want you to be careful because them streets ain't nothin' to play with. You don't know who's doin' what when they ain't around you. Always be watchin' yo' back and be aware of yo' surroundin's." A single tear rolled down mamma's flawless cheek. Just as she wiped her face, Jeremy reached in and kissed her. "I will mamma. I promise."

Could Heiresses' downfall be the start of a long overdue change for Jeremy? Would he finally stop contributing to many of momma's headaches and restless nights worryin' about her eldest and only son's extracurricular activities? She told the story to Jeremy with hopes of sendin' an important message. Her intentions were far from cruel. She only wanted Jeremy to realize that there were consequences that followed his actions. She needed Jeremy to understand that the streets didn't love him, nor did they care about how his family felt when he chose run them. It was her belief that if you lived a dangerous life, you were bound to die a tragic death.

Back At the House

"Girl, these ribs is finally done!" Sistah Beulah walked in with a stack of barbequed ribs waitin' to be marinated in mamma's special sauce. "Let me get that for you Ms. Beulah." Jeremy reached for the pan that seemed to make Sistah Beulah walk hunched over. "I got it Jeremy! You may wanna help Berry with all those bags she wrestlin' to get out of your lady friend's car. "She *finally* made it back hunh?" Momma chuckled at her own sarcasm. She knew when I shopped it took hours. I had to have everything coordinated and matchin' to a tee. It was how I'd been since I was old enough to dress myself.

Jeremy walked over and helped me grab my new wardrobe additions out of the back seat of Cassie's car. I was so happy to step onto familiar soil. "Damn Berry!" Jeremy was loud and indiscreet. "Did you manage to leave a few items for other shoppers?" Cassie snickered. "Whatever Jeremy! It's only four bags." I was irritated, yet glad to be home. "Thanks Cassie. I'll see you at the festivities tomorrow." I walked over and hugged her and whispered, "We'll talk more about *that* later." Cassie shook her head in acknowledgement. I had to find out more about this business venture she imposed on me. But, for now I just wanted to get in the shower and go to bed. I was still excited about turnin' sixteen, but just not as much as I was before I left. I walked in, kissed momma on the cheek, and spoke to sistah Beulah. "How was shoppin'?" Momma yelled as I was on my way up the stairs. "It went well! I'll tell you all about it tomorrow. Good night." I couldn't wait to hit the sack. Tomorrow couldn't come fast enough; but first I had to try on my new pieces. This way, if I wasn't satisfied or if I may need a different accessory, I could get up early enough to hit the mall before the party started. I hoped everything would come together. With all the shoppin' Cassie & I did, I didn't want to go anywhere *near* a clothin' store; al least for a couple of weeks.

The trip to the mall was exhausting as hell! Cassie and I searched high and low through the three story shopping center tryin' to find the apparel that complimented our curvaceous forms. She was on one end, and I was on the other. This was our way of tryin' not to pick the same item since our taste in clothin' was almost identical. We'd both decided that a separation would prove best in keepin' our outfits as unique as possible, even though this mall was frequented by a lot of our peers. But for the most part, we didn't have to worry about our peers showin' up dressed like our "twins" due to our financial status. Cassie and I knew we had to spend money and neither of us had a problem with it.

Ten stores and thirty pairs of shoes later, I finally found my top choice out of the selections I'd chosen throughout my four hour search. It was the perfect choice for a young lady comin' of age; at least that's what Cassie said when she gave her seal of approval outside my fittin' room. My perfect outfit came by way of the leather store on the second floor, six stores away from the famous pretzel shop I stopped at for my favorite large cheese pretzel.

I chose a royal blue jumper that hugged my hips as if it were painted onto my body. The straps were adjustable and trimmed in gold. My accessories would match perfectly considering the pocket on the front was stitched in gold. My still buddin', perky breasts made the front pocket curve in the right place. I chose a black, short sleeved, silk shirt to wear under it. Actually, I'd picked it up to compliment some tight Levi's I bought just because I wanted them. I knew when I went to the mall I wouldn't limit myself to just birthday apparel; with the wardrobe I already had, I kept my compulsive shoppin' to a minimum.

When I went into the dressin' room, Cassie entered the store scufflin' to get all six of her bags through the narrow entrance. I flagged her down from behind the dressin' room door. "Berry! You're just as bad as me. You haven't found anything yet?" She seemed out of breath while waitin' for a response. "Yeah! I said irritated. "I'm trying it on now. Tell me what you think." I walked out of the fitting room with my soon-to-be new clothes and socks on. There was a surrounding full sized mirror next to the room I came out of. I was delighted with my selection from every angle. I could tell by the men surroundin' the area where Cassie and I stood, that I was eye candy. "Damn baby!" One man that looked to be in his mid-twenties, stood behind us and blurted out his apparent satisfaction. I wasn't sure if his response was directed towards me or Cassie 'cuz Cassie had a nice physique; A bit more mature than mines. Everything she wore seemed tailor made. I stood there critiquin' and primpin' just to make sure this would be my final decision. By now I'd drawn a crowd of both males and females. I saw a couple of females frown and walk away whisperin' to one another, but the men continued with the gawkin' and sexist remarks. Although I loved the attention, I headed back into the room to disrobe without acknowledgin' one comment.

Tomorrow was now only about three hours away. Cassie and I were both exhausted, and after we made our last purchase we fled the mall like we were suspects in a high speed chase. After I finished "unpackin', I cleared my bags off my bed, put up my clothes and turned on my stereo. My eyes grew heavy and my body was tired. That's when I flopped across my bed where I would remain until I was awakened by the smell of biscuits, fried tomatoes and bacon the next mornin'.

Pre-Party Blues

The majority of the day I did what most teens do. I slept up until it was almost time for our guests to arrive. After eatin' a late breakfast with momma and Jeremy, I helped clear the dishes and straightened the kitchen as much as I could. There were servin' utensils, aluminum pans, and clean dishes waitin' to be put away from last night. Jeremy and momma decided to belt out the Happy Birthday tune, which to me sounded like two alley cats lickin' their wounds. It was a sweet gesture although they were off beat and vocally out of tune but comin' from them, it was just the way I liked it!

We all laughed and talked briefly about the party and who we thought would and wouldn't show up. It really didn't matter much to me, just as long as grandma and grandpa stopped by. Grandma was a jazzy little lady that always dressed nice and smelled good. She kept her salt and pepper hair and nails done and on any given day she may have her pistol in her purse. We knew when she had it 'cuz she carried her purse in a different way. Her hair was salt and pepper and she stood about five feet tall. Her dark complexion glowed in any climate. Momma reminded me so much of her, especially when she was upset or worried about somethin'. Granddad was more laid back. He was up on all the slang; old and new alike. He would do the latest handshakes with Jeremy and his friends. He stood six feet tall and had a flawless caramel color. He often told us stories about how he and grandma met. Each time I would sit and listen as if it were the first. Grandma and Granddad were the perfect match and I was their little precious Berry. I never could get away with my performances with them, but they spoiled me rotten anyway! But, when it was time to put me in check, grandma was the one to do the honors.

Anyhow, I couldn't wait to see them! I knew I was bound to get a special present from them. Last year they bought me a ceramic jewelry box with a merry-go-round on top. Whenever I was feelin' stressed out or just in one of my moods, I would wind it up and listen to the soft twinklin' music it played as it spun around. Although Jeremy gave me a gold watch, the jewelry box was the best gift I got just because my grandparents bought it. I couldn't wait for them to pull up. They rarely came over to the house. Momma would try to beat them to it by goin' over their house first in an effort to keep Jeremy's wrong doin' out of their faces. It worked thus far, but **today,** a quick visit wouldn't be heard of.

Jeremy asked if I wanted anything from the store as I approached the top stair headin' for my bedroom. "If it comes in the form of a sleepin' pill, I'll take it!" I smiled sheepishly at Jeremy as I leaned over the banister. My corny response made him chuckle. "Gone and get some rest girl. You'll need it for tonight." He winked at me and headed to the store to pick up some last minute items and Tylenol for momma.

Just as I put my fuzzy green slipper across the entrance of my doorway, "Berry?!" Momma was yellin' my name from the kitchen. "I hope she don't want me to come back downstairs," I thought to myself as I calmly answered, "Yes mom?" I took four steps from my doorway to the banister to hear her response.

"Please don't turn that music up too loud. My head is hurtin' and I gotta wait until Jeremy come back with my headache pills. Her headaches were beginnin' to surface more frequently like unwanted visitors. I was worried that she may need to go to the hospital but hoped that it would be tomorrow instead of today. Any day besides today! "When is your next doctor's appointment ma?" My concern showed through the wrinkles in my fore head. Although it was a special day for me, mother's health was way more important, so I quickly stepped out of my selfish thoughts. "Ain't no need to be worryin' yourself Berry. It ain't as bad as some of the other's I've had. I just want to get it under control before that D.J. come and start playin' even louder music than that stereo in your room. That's why I don't want you cuttin' it up all loud before Jeremy gets back." She evaded my question altogether like she often did when she wanted to avoid our line of questionin'. She would rather suffer with the pain than to worry Jeremy and me with her 'problems'.

"I won't momma. I'm about to go back to sleep anyway. Maybe you should take a rest too. It's not like you have anything else to do." Momma peeked her head out of the kitchen and looked at me with her eyes squinted. "I got a lot to do, thank you very much! I'm tryin' to get finished so it won't be a whole lot tonight."

What could she possible have left to do besides put the mac and cheese in the oven with the rolls? Our house stayed clean. There wasn't a piece of dust or dirt in sight. Momma would clean the paint off the walls if she could scrub any harder. I cleaned the bathroom and mopped the hallway before Cassie and I went shoppin' on yesterday, Jeremy and

Angelo raked the yard and got up the blowin' sales papers two days ago, and the three of us had just finished cleanin' the kitchen. But, this was how momma kept her mind and thoughts peaceful. When she was depressed or anxious, she cleaned. This definitely wouldn't be a trait for me to pick up; at least I hoped it wouldn't!

I woke up from my extended nap around 7:28 p.m. I couldn't believe I'd slept that long. Although it felt good it made me feel groggy. I reached for the power button on the stereo until I thought about momma's request from earlier that day. I went into the bathroom and began to draw my bath before I headed downstairs to check on momma.

Jeremy was nowhere in sight as I passed his unusually clean bedroom. Momma must have cleaned it while I was sleepin'. I crept to the entrance of Momma's bedroom where I quietly opened the door. I was tryin' not to disturb her just in case she was still asleep; *IF* she'd decided to take a nap after all. As I opened the door to take a peek in, moma sneaked up behind me. "You were lookin' for me?" Momma was standin' there with her hands on her hips. Her hair was down and bent on the ends. She wore a cute pink soft cotton sweater/blouse with a pair of *Levi 501* jeans that hugged her toned butt. She had a green apron on that read: *kiss the cook*; so I did! I gave her the biggest kiss my lips could muster and I hugged her as if it were my last time seein' her. She looked so pretty and well rested. "How's your headache?" She looked at me and smiled like she was shocked that I was concerned. "It'll be back if you don't go and start getting' ready before your guests arrive." I could take a hint. She'd be yellin' at me in a minute so I hurried to the bathroom to check my water. On my way up the stairs I let momma know that I loved her and how pretty she looked tonight.

I was beginning to get caught up in my emotions. I mean, she and Jeremy did all of this for me. I couldn't help but feel emotional that I made it to see sixteen, and that I was fortunate enough to have a family to spend it with; let alone the party of my dreams. A lot of kids my age didn't have that option, so I had to feel appreciative of all that they'd done for me; not only today, but every day. I guess my maturity started kickin' in sometime while I was sleepin'.

I went in my room, cut on the stereo, took out my new ensemble and laid it across the bed along with the sexy thong and matching bra I would wear. My jewelry and perfume would add the finishin' touches. *"Excuse me Dougie Fresh you're on… on, on, on!* I sang along with the radio as I gathered my robe and toothbrush, and headed for the tub. The water was hot as hell……just like I liked it!

By the time I got out of the tub it was now 8:45 p.m. and cars were startin' to pull up in the driveway. The first person to arrive was Sistah Beulah. She had Damon with her helpin' to take a few bags outta the car. It looked as if she'd come with even more food to add to the buffet we already had downstairs. I remember thinkin' to myself, "Even if people don't have a good time, at least they can say they ate good!" That would be my defense if I heard anybody talk negative about my party. My response would be, "But yo' greedy ass ate didn't you?"

The radio was now bumpin', *"I Need Love"* by L.L. Cool J as I went back to my room to get dressed. Now that's who I wish were at my party tonight. I definitely wouldn't be a virgin if he showed up! Although he wasn't as cute as

DeAngelo and some of the other guys that frequented our house with Jeremy, L.L. was so damn sexy with those juicy ass lips! Anyway, I proceeded to get dressed. I took my time purposely so that I could make my grand entrance. This way everybody could lay their eyes on me at the same time. Cassie taught me that.

I looked myself over in the full body mirror that embraced my closet door and I have to say, I was pleased with the sight of the reflection that gazed sheepishly back at me. I couldn't believe that I was finally the young women I had longed to become. Not to mention a fine ass young women at that. I wasn't conceded, but I had to give myself props because that jumpsuit was like no other outfit I'd bought before. Usually I would wear my tight jeans with a loose fitting shirt or blouse, or one that would come down just enough to cover my butt. I was always a little self-conscience about the type of clothes I wore, although I had the finest and latest selections to choose from. Plus momma and Jeremy critiqued me often. If I had on jeans that complimented my shape or wore a skirt that was too high over my knees, Jeremy would make me go right back in the house and change. If it weren't him, it was momma once I would come down the stairs to go to school. What's funny is that these were clothes that *they'd* either bought or took me shoppin' to pick out.

"Hey Birthday Girl!" Sistah Beulah glanced up from the livin' room and saw me comin' down the stairs. She opened her arms for me to come and give her a hug. "Girl, look at them thighs! If you don't slow down you gone mess around and have a butt like mines!" I knew she didn't mean any harm by that, but if she knew the remarks that people made behind her back, she would understand why her comment was boarder line insultin' to me. Don't get me wrong, sistah Beulah did have a big butt, but that's all it was. She had no shape or curves; just this gigantic ass that people saw jiggle up and down when she moved. It didn't help that her name was 'Beulah' either. Big, bouncy-butt Beulah was what the kids called her. They would mimic thunder sounds when she would take steps through the church and swooshing noises in reference to her stockin's rubbin' together when she walked. Yeah, the other women may have talked about her, but *somebody* liked her 'cuz she damn sure had six kids that she didn't make by herself!

"Well, I ain't gone wait to give you yo' gift. I want mines to be the first gift of the night." She reached into her tattered brown leather purse that coordinated with the long brown corduroy skirt and black sequined blouse she wore. She handed me an envelope. "Thank you Sistah Beulah!" I accepted graciously.

"Open it up Berry! She was excited like she didn't know what was in the envelope. Sweet Sixteen; read the front of the card with a flower pattern engraved on it. There was a garden and the flowers were painted in beautiful reds, greens and yellows. The inside of the card read: *Happy Birthday on a day that is just as sweet as you!* There were two twenties stuffed inside and the card was signed individually by her kids, including Myron! My eyes started to water. I was over whelmed with emotion, but I didn't want the trace of eyeliner I wore to smear. *Happy Sweet Sixteen Berry. I hope your day is filled with all you desire. - Myron* ☺

Even though it touched me that sistah Beulah gave it a

thought to buy me a card, it was the note from Myron that touched me the most. He was always so nice to me. I did notice that Mitchell's name wasn't anywhere on my card. It was straight though because I never cared for him anyway. I thanked Sistah Beulah again and gave her another hug. I appreciated her gift just as much as I did the other gifts I received throughout the course of the night. I wanted to inquire about when Myron would be home, but I wasn't really tryin' to get the gossip started. Unlike sistah Beulah, I never let people know my business. After a while, I started lookin' forward to the made-up stories people told about me. They gave me way more credit then I actually deserved! But, what the hell? I took it all in stride!

Let's Get This Party Started

By 10 o'clock the yard was packed. It wasn't quite at its full seatin' capacity, but not far from it. From the look of it, the party would be standin' room only within the next hour or so. As I glanced around the yard there were a lot of familiar faces. Outside of the normal crowd that Jeremy socialized with on a regular basis, there were also attendees from the hood that we grew up with; either people that still stayed within the vicinity or those that moved away but still kept in touch from time to time.

I noticed three or four females from the high school cheerleadin' squad that wanted to so badly recruit me in my sophomore year. I wasn't a fool though. I knew that they just wanted to be in the imaginary circle that they somehow created for me. It was more of a popularity technique gone wrong. They figured if they hung around me, they would be able to meet Jeremy and the rest of the fella's. Little did they know that their plan would backfire. I ended up goin' to one of their practices in the gym one day. They just *knew* I was gone sign up. At the end of practice they had the boo-boo faces when I 'politely' declined due to 'other' social engagements I had to attend. Those engagements that took place right in the livin' room as I watched my favorite dance show called "The Scene" and all of my other favorite shows. Nevertheless, they were now at the party lookin' around and tryin' to be noticed by the guys. One girl even started doin' cheer kicks and the splits. "Some hoes will do anything for attention", I thought to myself.

By now, word had made it all through the neighboring areas that a backyard party was goin' on over the way, on McKinley. Many people knew when they heard the street name that it was the McDaniel's house. And those that didn't know us personally had definitely heard of my brother. That's just how popular Jeremy was; more so because he shared the same name as my dad. Many of the gang bangers from our parents' era that knew or socialized with my parents, now had children tryin' to imitate the many stories their parents told them. I can honestly say that the majority of people that came to our party knew of us and heard good things about us. These were the people that respected my parents at one point or another. That's one reason why they let their kids come to the party at our house in the first place. And then you had the other people. Either those that know you and respect you for who you are, or those fake ass people that just came for the freebie eatin' and drinkin'. We had a whole corner of them in our yard that night. It definitely wasn't hard to figure out who they were; they kept a plate of food or a drink in their hands all night!

Angelo had the sounds bumpin'. Chaka Khan screamed *Through the Fire* out of the 200 watt Pioneer speakers he'd set up around the four corners of the yard. "This song is dedicated to Ms. McDaniel with her fly self." Momma smiled at the compliment Angelo threw at her as he switched into the next song by *Earth, Wind, and Fire.* "Hey Birthday girl!" One of my male classmates, Drew, was standin' on the gate as I walked past. I was flattered to see him there. Drew was a cutie that would always go out of his way to make sure I was straight in school. If he heard anybody talkin' junk about me or Jeremy, he would "cap" on them somethin' awful. He definitely had jokes, and none of them were the same. People would avoid him in the hallway for fear of him gettin' laughs at their expense. "Hey Drew!" I put my plastic cup of Momma's 'special' punch on the closest table I saw and gave him a big hug. I hadn't seen him in a couple of semesters and wondered what happened to him. Rumor around the school was that he hustled in the streets so hard that he ended up with enough money to open up about five "spots" sporadically placed over on the northwest side of the city. It wasn't hard to see his progress. His jewelry sparkled like it was sunny outside. He pulled out a one hundred dollar bill and pinned it on my overall pocket along with the other bills I'd accumulated that night. "That is so sweet! Thanks Drew!" I showed gratitude for his generosity. "When you comin' back to school?" Drew looked shocked at my question. "Awwww! I didn't know you cared Berry!" I felt a wise crack comin' on, but apparently he was serious about what he'd just said. He told me he'd thought that I didn't like him because I rarely said anything to him. I had to get him to realize that I never really kicked it with anyone in our class, nor in the school for that matter. "Damn! I forgot your little Indian girl lookin' ass was mean as hell! I hated when people called me mean. I couldn't understand why it was so mean for me to just stay to myself. It kept me from bein' pulled into unnecessary bullshit that people stirred up. I was *not* tryin' to get caught up in any of the hood news gossip. It also kept people out of my business. There was no need for me to draw attention to myself. Jeremy took care of that all by himself. The highlight of the school day was the usual who got into a fight over who? Who got shot or jacked for their shoes? Who sold drugs and who was sleepin' with who? I didn't care about none of that shit. Who was I to judge? "So, are you seeing anybody?" Just as I was about to answer, "Could I please have the birthday girl over by the DJ booth?" Angelo spoke as if he were irritated. I told Drew that I would be right back and headed over to Angelo. I remember gigglin' and thinkin' to myself, "My man is so jealous!"

"This is a special night for a special person who I am very fond of. Her brother is my "boy" and her mother is like my second mother because she s shows me mad love." Angelo winked at moma and continued to speak into the mic. "Let's all lift our glasses to this beautiful young lady who we all came here to celebrate with." He looked me in my eyes like we were the only two people there. Everyone with a cup, glass, or forty ounce of "eight ball" beer raised their hands to toast me. My eyes began to well with tears. This would be a night I would never forget.

I was so buzzed off the punch I wanted to cry. I just felt so emotional. But, I refused to shed a tear. My eyeliner wasn't about to run and smear my reputation. "Happy Birthday Berry!" Everybody in the yard yelled it on key together as Angelo pumped the crowd with Salt & Pepa's *Express Yo'self*. The crowd was hype and everybody started to sing along. "So....you havin' fun?" Angelo whispered in my ear as I stood next to him lookin' through his album collection. "Yea, this is straight! Come on and work that bo-dy!" I sang along with Pepa as I signified. "You know you look good tonight, right?" Angelo moved in a little closer. I noticed he was lookin' around as he inched his way over to me. He was makin' sure Jeremy and momma weren't within eye or earshot as he stalked his prey. "It's about time," I thought to myself. I wouldn't run. My *goal* was to be caught. "Do I?" My voice lowered an octave as I answered "my man's" question. I gave him direct eye contact. I wanted him to see my interest in his flirtatious conversation. At this point I was ready for whatever he had his mind on. Hopefully the drinks hadn't altered my thinkin' and this would be the night Cassie spoke of on our way to the mall. It better be as good as she said it would be or I was gone have some words for her ass tomorrow.

Speaking of Cassie, I hadn't seen her since about an hour or so ago when she was standin' next to Jeremy feedin' him a piece of chicken. "Where's Jeremy?" Angelo was checkin' through the LP's and tapes for his next plastic ballot. "I was just wondering the same thing about Cassie." I replied as I tilted my freshened up cup towards my mouth. "They may be doin' something I wish we could be doin!" Angelo smiled at me sneakily. I blushed and sipped simultaneously as I responded in my sexy voice, "And what might that be?" Just as Angelo was about to answer, "Hey man! Where yo' bath-er-room at?" Some man with disheveled hair and oily mechanic overalls staggered his way over to where Angelo and I stood. He wobbled and bumped into the DJ table. "Hey dog!" Angelo was irritated. "The bathroom is any tree you can find outside of this yard. Get the fuck on!"

Momma had just walked back to where Angelo & I were. She's been out in the front of the house talkin' with sistah Beulah. I guess the music was startin' to bother her. "Berry? Go in the house and get a knife so we can start cuttin' the cake. It's almost one o'clock; these folk need to go home!" The party had just started to get hyped. "Aww ma! The

D'Aviér

party is just gettin' started." I whined like I was turnin' ten again. "Girl! Go get somethin' to cut this cake with so these people can be on they way." Sistah Beulah chimed in, "They ain't got to go home, but they got to get the hell outta here!" Momma and sistah Beulah snickered at that corny ass comment. If I didn't know any better, I'd swear the two of them had been in the punch bowl more than me. "I turned to walk towards the back door when I noticed Jeremy comin' from the garage with Damon. "Where you goin' Berry? Jeremy stopped in front of me and kissed me on my forehead. "In the house to get a knife. Momma is ready for the party to be over." Jeremy wasn't payin' me the slightest attention. He was too busy scopin' the yard to check things out......once again. He did this all the time. My brother was alwaaays aware of his surroundings. It didn't matter if he was in the house or out in the streets, that's just how he was.

When I went to the kitchen drawer to get the cake cutter, I saw Cassie standin' in the livin' room with her arms folded like she was unsettled! "What did Jeremy do now?" I asked myself as I snickered at the thought of the answer to my question. Jeremy does some of the dumbest shit to irritate a person. As I walked closer I noticed she was talkin' with Calvin. Remember Calvin? My dad's friend that always had a different woman? He'd stopped by to wish me a happy birthday and give me a few dollars. He had on a pair of nice brown slacks with a shiny orange shirt exposin' his chest hairs. His Lagerfield cologne filled the room. We hadn't seen him in a while. Momma thought that he'd finally settled down with one of his many lady friends but that was furthest from the truth.

The conversation ended abruptly when I walked in the

room. There was this awkward silence and they both just stood there lookin' at me as if they did somethin' sneaky. Cassie eye's looked red like she'd been cryin'. But then again, with as much punch as I drank, everybody's eyes looked red. I quickly dismissed my suspicion and blamed it on the alcohol. "What's wrong with y'all?" Calvin smiled and gave me a fake punch in the arm. "You enjoyin' yo' night Berry?" He evaded my question. "I need to go upstairs and freshen my make-up." Cassie looked for an excuse to leave the room. She practically ran up the stairs into the bathroom. "Well, I guess I'd better be goin' kiddo. I got a hot date tonight!"

Calvin headed towards the kitchen so he could leave through the back door. Just as he was attempting to leave, Jeremy walked in. "Aww man, you about to go?" Calvin and Jeremy slapped hands. "Yeah man, Calvin responded. "I got's to go freshen up for some business I got on the floor. You know how that go!" Jeremy nodded his head in agreement. "Ay man? I was wonderin' if you could just hold on so I can toast Berry and get this party wrapped up; where she at anyway?" Calvin pointed towards the livin' room. "Jeremy! Here man. Calvin reached into his back pocket and grabbed a card. "Take my business card."

Jeremy's eyes bucked out in shock. The front of the card that Calvin gave him had a nude picture of Tirianna on the front of it! "So the rumors are true hunh?" Calvin looked at Jeremy like he was crazy. "What rumors man? The one's about her bein' a hoe? Some of it *is* but *most* of it ain't. Calvin spoke matter-of-factly. "It's true that she's a hoe, but she ain't just *any* hoe, she's *my* hoe. Jeremy smiled and the two of them clapped hands again. "Man, all these years I wondered why you had so many different women. They was all 'tight' too. Now I know!

Calvin was bein' idolized by my brother. "So you ready to make some more money?" Calvin pulled out a stack of money that was as big as a Whopper at Burger King. I walked in the kitchen as he put it back in his pocket. I was checkin' myself out in the mirrors that lined the back livin' room wall. I had to make sure everything was still lookin' straight. "We'll definitely be in touch man." Calvin winked at Jeremy and went back to the party. Angelo continued to hype the crowd with *Somebody's Watching Me* by Maxwell. Jeremy walked over to the disc jockey table and whispered something to Angelo. The music went off. "If everybody who doesn't have a cup would please get a drink so the family can toast the birthday girl." Angelo yelled through the microphone. People scrambled to the punch bowl that momma and Sistah Beulah refilled about three times now. Some picked up their forty bottles and toasted after they spilled some on the ground for their "homies" that didn't make it. Crash! Everybody in the yard turned towards the noise. It was one of the cheerleaders laid out on the grass. Her drunk ass tried to break her fall by pullin' the table cloth. All the dirty plates filled with chicken bones and half eaten mashed potatoes came tumblin' down on her. Some guys standin' in the corner of the yard were all too anxious to help her up as they laughed and tried to cop a few feels. Momma ran over to make sure she was alright.

"O.K., some of you need to put your cups down!" Angelo joked as he passed the mic to Jeremy.

Cassie reappeared in he crowd. She took her place next to Jeremy as he cleared his throat. Momma made her way back to the table and stood opposite Cassie. "To my little sister Berry turnin' sixteen today. It seems like just yesterday I was walkin' her to school. I remember when she would come out the bathroom butt naked and ask me to put her clothes on." The guys in the back started whistlin' and howlin' like dogs. I punched Jeremy and hid my face behind my hands with embarrassment. "Hey! That's my sister. Don't make me put nobody out! Jeremy lowered his glass and looked through the crowd with a serious face. "Like I was sayin'!" Jeremy picked up where he left off. "I remember when I used to pull you in my red wagon so you could get one of those free lunches the government used to give out. Now you're sixteen and tryin' to tell me what to do! I love you little Berry." Jeremy hugged me tight, kissed me on my forehead, and headed towards the garage.

Momma started the second toast. She told me she was proud of me and how I've grown into the beautiful young women she'd hoped to live to see and a bunch of other mushy stuff. She maintained her composure although she was feelin' her buzz. She looked towards the back for Jeremy as DeAngelo asked to crowd to "Give it up for Berry on her sweet sixteen birthday."

Just as the applause started, Jeremy came up to the front pullin' the wagon he spoke about during the toast. The same wagon he used to pull me in when he delivered papers! There was a two-tiered, pink and white marbled cake inside of it that read: *Happy Sixteenth Birthday Berry*. The wagon was in mint condition and Jeremy had it repainted with my name spelled out in gold letters on the side. He had tiny little white walled tires put on it that covered the gold spoke wheel frames he'd bought. There wasn't a hint of rust to prove the wagons true age. The tears ran uncontrollably down both Jeremy's and my face. He even had momma wash the teddy bear that tagged along with us to the few houses in the neighborhood where he occasionally deliver papers to. I ran and hugged my brother so tight! This was the best gift ever! It was like Jeremy was attemptin' to save one of his fondest childhood memories of him and me. Momma came over and hugged us both. She presented me with "Cookie", the bear I named after the blue monster who demolished cookies on my favorite show, *Sesame Street*. She'd tied two pink ribbons on the ears to give it a more feminine look. All we heard were awwwwww's from the crowd. I think I may have actually seen a few people wipe away a tear or two.

"Let's give it up for Berry and the McDaniel family as we rock the party with a few more songs." Angelo played the Beastie Boys and further exited the crowd. Momma and Jeremy unloaded the cake and put it on the table they reserved for me. "Pssst!" Angelo motioned for me to join him near the back entrance while he started packin' up his album collection. I obliged. "So? You feel sixteen yet?" He licked his big brown lips suggestively as he waited for my answer. My heart started beatin' fast and sweat started to bead on my forehead. I knew I couldn't let him see me sweat. This is the night I've been waitin' for and the man that could get the job done. I focused on his sexy ass lips as he sat on the back stairs and pulled me over to stand between his legs. He was definitely playin' with fire. "So, you goin' to bed after the party?" I frowned at his remark and tried to sound as grown as I could. "Naw boy! I ain't goin' to bed. You tryin' to say I'm a little girl?" De Angelo smirked. "I can tell you ain't little!" He looked me up and down. His hazel eyes pierced through my clothes straight to my heart. "Little girls don't have bodies like this. Damn Berry!" DeAngelo grabbed his dick and caressed it. "Look what you done did!" My eyes got ten times their normal size. The bulge in his pants was HUGE! I *had* to touch it to believe it. I reached for it and drew my hand back with fear. "You can't be scared of it baby." He took my hand and put it in his buldgin' lap as he moved it back and forth. My pussy was soaked. I was ready to be "touched" right there on the back stairs. Just as Angelo moved in to kiss me, there was commotion in the yard.

SMACK!!! "Don't you ever put yo' fuckin' hands on me!" It was momma's voice I heard. She was talkin' to the drunk man that Angelo had words with earlier. He'd tried to holler at moma and hit her on the butt. I jumped up and headed towards the front. When I looked up, Angelo was in front of me. "Man, get the fuck out of here! Jeremy flew from behind the table and started swingin' on the drunk man. Once Angelo moved, all the guys in the yard fell into position. Damon pushed Sistah Beulah toward the back door and started fightin'. I ran into the house to get a knife. I knew Jeremy had ammo, but that was the one thing he never let me in on: neither the location nor how to use it. Apparently the drunk man had partners in place as well. There were about three other men in the yard all dressed in the same mechanic overalls fightin' with Jeremy and his boys.

Momma came in the house just as I was headed back into the yard to help my brother. "Go back in the house Berry!" She yelled at the top of her lungs. "Call the police

Beulah." Sistah Beulah ran into the livin' room and grabbed the rotary phone off the end table. Momma ran right past her into her bedroom. When she reappeared, she had a black carbine rifle loaded and cocked. "Momma No!" I yelled and tried to grab her arm, but she pushed me back and yanked her arm away. When she went out the door, I went right after her with the knife she told me to put down. I ran ahead of her as she aimed the rifle in the air. SLICE!!! I cut the guy that kicked Jeremy as he tried to get off the ground. He grabbed his lacerated cheek. "You Bitch!" He came after me. When Damon saw him headed towards me, Whap! He hit the man across the head with one of the metal folded chairs. Knocked him out cold! Jeremy's crew started mobbin' the other crew. It was like somethin' out of a movie! Angelo was standin' next to me after he socked some guy in his jaw. "You alright?" He checked me over. BLOOM! Momma shot the rifle in the air in an effort to get things under control. The drunk man lay on the ground right next to the D.J booth moanin' and holdin' his chest.

Angelo went over and stood next to him. "You hurt man?" He stuck his hand out like he was gone help the guy up off the ground. Just as the man reached for Angelo's hand, he kicked him in his side. "Now you should be hurt mutha fucka!" I walked up and looked down at the man who seemed to be helpless. He whispered somethin'. "What yo' punk ass say?" Angelo bent down to hear what the drunk had to say. Just as he bent over, we could hear police sirens comin' our way.

"Yo cuzin!" The man whispered to Angelo. "What about my cuzin nigga?" The drunk hesitated. "He told me to give you this." He pulled his hand out of his overalls and pointed a .38 special to Angelo's head and pulled the trigger. I stood there in shock. Angelo fell to the ground. His brain matter on my pants leg and splattered all over my shoes. ANGELO! I screamed at the top of my lungs. Jeremy and Damon rushed to my side stompin' the man unconscious. By this time the police rushed in the yard with their pistols drawn, they found me screamin' and hollerin' erratically, a man beat and bleedin' from the mouth while momma performed cpr, and Angelo dead in a pool of his own blood.... Damn!

D'Aviér

If Tomorrow Never Comes

If tomorrow never comes...
Try to hold back the flowing tears
For we knew this day would come
God has been preparing us for years

If tomorrow never comes...
I don't want any of you to mourn
Instead, rejoice at my "home going"
Remember how happy you were
On that autumn day that I was born

If tomorrow never comes...
Remember all that I stood for
And never let go of your faith
Remember my sense of humor; my smile
Although you will no longer see my face
But breathe a sigh of relief
Because now I am in a better place

If tomorrow never comes...
Have faith that I am not alone
Know that in spirit I am still here
And that only the outer shell is gone
For now I am with my Savior
As He has called for me to come home
D'Aviér

Days to Weeks; Weeks to Months.....

Life seemed to accelerate over the next few years. Jeremy was in and out of the house more frequently, and his excessive groomin' was now becomin' untamed. He and Calvin became closer and started hangin' out damn near every weekend. He would pick Jeremy up sometimes Friday afternoon after work, and they wouldn't be seen until late Saturday night or early Sunday mornin'. Cassie seemed to be irritated with the newfound relationship between the two of them. Jeremy would reassure her that it was more business than anything. "He's so much older than you Jeremy. What could the two of you possibly have in common?" Cassie would fuss about it but once Calvin came around, she camouflaged her emotions very well.

I ended up graduatin' from high school with honors. After the party I became even more popular than before. For some odd reason, people wanted to be in my circle now more than ever. Sex became second nature, although my first experience was well after high school. I turned my virginity over to this guy named Andrew, a cousin of Cassie's. We were introduced a few months after the shootin' incident at the party. Momma and Jeremy both thought it would be a good way to take my mind off of it. We ended up kickin' it briefly, but after a year into the relationship we went our separate ways. Andrew ended up enlisting in the Navy and was stationed somewhere over in Idaho. He and I remained good friends over the years and I would often joke with him about bringin' back some of those good ass Idaho potatoes!

We would go out on platonic dates whenever he came back to Detroit on leave. Our conversations always turned into "what if's". The usual what if we'd stayed together? What if we got married and had children? We both knew that it would never happen though. Besides, I don't think he would have been too thrilled if he found out about my evening job that Cassie turned me on to.

Before I met Andrew, depression came over me like a cloud on a rainy day. I couldn't stop thinkin' about seein' Angelo layin' there dead in our yard. I cried almost every day up until the funeral which took place the week after my party. The only reason I didn't cry then was because of the antidepressant med's I was given by our doctor. I was too high at the funeral. It took me a while to get myself together, but I made it over the hump. I took Angelo's death as a sign for me to live. His unnecessary murder changed my whole outlook on life.

The funeral was actually sadder than the shootin' itself. His grandmother had him decked out though. Angelo's casket was made like the Mercedes he drove and was the same color. He was dressed in a denim Levi hook up with a Kangol that matched his white Izod shirt. Jeremy, Damon and a few of the other home boys dressed like him. There were two funeral cars reserved just for flowers alone.

We eventually found out that Angelo was set up by his cousin. Rumor had it that the cousin shorted him some merchandise and severely suffered DeAngelo's wrath. His wired jaw and hospital visit caused him to lose his job at the skatin' rink on 8 mile as a result. Angelo beat him up when he said he wouldn't DJ my party for free. The cousin ended up sendin' some guys to my party to pay Angelo back. In *no way* was he expectin' for things to end up the way they did; or so he claimed.

During the funeral Angelo's grandmother passed out after she tried to lift Angelo up out of the casket. Her son and nephew grabbed her and tried to calm her down, but she fell out. She had everybody in the church crying hysterically. Even Pastor Elkins was choked up.

A few days after the funeral Angelo's grandmother's house was raided. There were police officers everywhere. It was said that they confiscated all different types of guns, money, and drugs. Angelo's grandmother was hauled off in handcuffs and later sentenced to three years in a women's federal prison. Jeremy said she got that amount of time because the Fed's weren't really for certain if the items belonged to her or Angelo before he died. Some people around the hood claim that the cousin snitched as a way to escape charges for puttin' a 'hit' out on Angelo. He's supposedly in a witness protection program hidin' from both *his* family and the man he sent that actually did the shootin'. The grandmother was eventually released from prison, but no one ever saw her in church or around the neighborhood again. Her house went up for sale about three weeks later.

Momma took a likin' to this deacon in church named Mr. Wilbert Monroe. They would go to various church programs and to feed the animals out at Belle Isle off Jefferson. Deacon Monroe really made momma happy. I hadn't seen her this giddy since Jeremy and I were little. Mr. Monroe wasn't really much of a looker, but he had a wonderful personality and a matchin' sense of humor. Momma was always laughin' when they talked on the phone or visited one another. Overall, he put fun back into momma's life. Somethin' she refused to do often unless it involved draggin' Jeremy and I with her.

I couldn't find one thing to complain about when it came to Mr. Monroe. He was always concerned with how my day was or whatever was on my mind. Jeremy didn't want to like him at first, but eventually he gave in once he realized how content momma was when the deacon was around. As long as nothin' was said about his business at hand, he was straight. The two of them ultimately broke up after Mr. Monroe tried to convince momma to take her key from Jeremy and give it to him. He was appalled with the way Jeremy was allowed to come and go as he pleased. "He's a grown man Brandy! He shouldn't even be living here; let alone coming and going all times of the night. The devil comes in many forms Brandy." Momma argued back, "He's my son Wilbert! I won't turn my back on my son. I can't let you live in the house his father left us." Deacon Monroe didn't like the fact that momma didn't see things his way. "His father is dead Brandy. You have to move on and live life for yourself. Berry and Jeremy are adults now. Let me be all the man you need." Momma was silent. "Either we expand on our relationship Brandy, or let it go." At this point, I don't think Wilbert realized that he'd just clearly fucked up and ended the relationship hisself. Momma didn't take very kindly to ultimatums. Besides that, Jeremy and I were her life. She lived to take care of us in some form or another. Momma would never forsake her happiness with us for Mr. Monroe's old ass, nor anyone else for that matter. The more Jeremy and I needed her, the more she felt needed. She didn't want to be taken care of after daddy died. Takin' care of me and Jeremy made momma busy. She *wanted* to cook and clean for us 'cuz it gave her somethin' to do.

Needless to say, Mr. Monroe was no more. Momma didn't show many emotions behind the breakup either. At least not around Jeremy and me. Apparently, she was on to Mr. Monroe's request to move in before he even said it. She never admitted it, but I knew she was aware he just needed a place to stay. Before he started kickin' it with momma he was rentin' a room in Pastor Elkins basement.

"What's up kiddo? You ready for this charity event tonight?" Cassie called to make sure I was on point. She seemed more excited than I was about my next client. She'd arranged for us to meet at one of the hotels located in Southfield, a suburb of Detroit. "About as ready as I'll ever be." I sighed after my sarcastic response. "What's wrong Berry? You're not about to start that bullshit about there has to be more in life than this are you?" Cassie was irritated by my on again off again attitude towards my disguised profession. When I was first introduced to this new opportunity, I was excited about it. There was a sense of satisfaction knowin' that I would be my *own* boss, in a sense. This allowed me the opportunity to make my *own* money, help momma out with the bills, shop my ass off without Jeremy *rationing out* his money in bits and pieces amongst other shit. Jeremy had really started gettin' tight with the money. It was only if we *really* needed stuff that determined *if* he would get it, but the unlimited shoppin' sprees ended quite abruptly some time ago. His excuse every other week was that there was a temporary drought and business was slow.

Momma thought I was workin' at the bar over on

Fenkell and Greenlawn with Cassie. I hated lyin' to her, but Cassie said this was the only way to justify my late night rendezvous'. If momma and Jeremy found out, we'd both be dead. All this time Cassie deceived my brother he didn't have one inclination of her past. I guess all that mattered to him was that she was there whenever he needed her; and she was. Well, except for the night Angelo's death. She'd been feelin' sick and ended up leavin' after we cut the cake. She was completely unaware of the next events that would take place after she'd left. Cassie didn't find out until the next afternoon when she came over and saw the yellow police tape surroundin' the yard. Neither Jeremy not I called her that night' it was just too much goin' on.

I continued talkin' while I put on my lipstick. "I'm not startin' shit Cassie!" My eyes rolled beyond the top of my head. "I know the routine. I've been doin' this for a while now. So, is he as cute in person as he is on his picture?" My curiosity was aroused. Butterflies took over my stomach. Cassie snickered at my juvenile anxiety. "He's even cuter! You're not nervous, are you?" I put up a front, "Of course not. I just wanted to know what to expect." We ended the conversation after we solidified our meetin' arrangements.

It just wouldn't register in my head why this sexy ass man needed me to escort him to this event. I knew he had a hood fan club, yet he chose an escort service to get a date? What was I about to get myself into? Over the past few months I'd had my share of weirdo's. There was a man that wanted me to scratch his back until it started bleedin', a couple of requests to moan extra loud and a lot of other weird ass suggestions. There was even one that wanted to be whipped! I'll admit, I did do that shit! It was just something kinky about havin' a nigga beg for you to smack his ass, but I do have morals! I refused to have oral sex with anyone. I didn't care how much they offered to pay. My mouth wasn't goin' on no dirty ass dick that had been God knows where. And nobody's dirty dick was goin' in my butt either. There were a few that got mad because I wouldn't let them do that shit, but oh well. It was two things I didn't sell; my soul and my booty hole!

My list of clientele included a city councilman's son and a couple of star college basketball players. There were a couple of very low profile lawyers I hooked up with, both defense attorneys. That would prove to be beneficial if Jeremy ever got into trouble. The majority of my 'dates' were dealers though. I'd been around street distributors basically all my life, so Cassie started me out based on my surroundin's. Who knew they'd be willin' to pay with all the females that practically threw the pussy at them?

Nevertheless, this profession was becomin' tiresome. Yeah, the money was straight and I liked goin' different places, but I dreaded the after parties that only included me and the men I escorted that evenin'. I was tired of playin' acrobatic; twistin' and turnin' my body into all kinds of different positions tryin' to fulfill some of their weird ass requests.

There was this one guy I escorted to an event down at Cobo Hall located off Jefferson in Downtown Detroit. He was crazy as hell! The date started off really well. He seemed to be such a gentleman as we walked around and conversed with a few of his colleagues that supported his artwork. He opened doors for me and grabbed my hand as we strolled through the display gallery. He acted as if we'd known each other for years. When different people came up to congratulate him on his latest pieces, he'd introduce me as his very good friend, Berry. His name was Corey, and he was very attractive and business-like. He spoke proper and smelled like a fragrance that came straight out of a magazine. I was truly impressed by his work and knowledge of art. That was until about the third scotch he drank started to kick in.

Corey became more aggressive and belligerent as the night progressed and his guests started to leave. He took me to this cheesy ass, shabby motel on Clairmount, right off the Lodge freeway. This was one of my first clients that Cassie turned me on to, so I wasn't really sure of what to expect. I don't really think she did either, 'cuz this was just the beginnin' of her branchin' off into her own escort service. But even with that taken into consideration, I couldn't believe that this was where he expected for us to end our night.

"Ummm, I'm not really comfortable about this place Corey. Can we go somewhere else?" I tried to be as polite as possible; tryin' not to exhibit my fear. "Shut up bitch and get the fuck out!" He got out and slammed his door. I don't know why my silly ass thought he was about to walk around and open the door for me like he'd been doin' all night, but I kind of sat there waitin' for him to come around to my side. He just stood there with this dumb ass look on his face. I hesitated openin' the door, but I got out and clutched my purse as I headed towards the entrance of the motel.

Once Corey finally stumbled to the front door, he grabbed my arm and pushed me into the room. I ended up breakin' a heel and bitin' my lip as a result of his forcefulness. "This bastard done lost his damn mind! This is going to be a fucked up night for somebody!" I thought to myself as I touched my bottom lip. I knew I was gone try my best to make sure it wasn't me that suffered. I got into ghetto mode real quick. I knew I had my blade in my purse, but I had to strategize how I was gone cut his ass. Clearly he was drunk and abusive, so I knew I had to play the game in order to get out of this situation alive.

He walked around the bed after he came out of the bathroom and started takin' off his clothes. Damn! His naked body was tight as hell! But his mind was twisted. He had to be nuts if he actually thought I was about to fuck him. This was one time I did not care about not getting' paid by a client. And if Cassie had somethin' to say about it, then her dingy actin' ass could come back and sleep with this maniac herself!

"Well, are you just gone stand there lookin' at your face, or come give my money's worth?" I walked slowly towards the bed. That's it bitch! Come get up on this." He rubbed his dick to keep his erection. I have to say, the brother had it goin' on! If he wasn't drunk and ignorant the night could have been well worth it. I got on the bed and leaned towards him. He yanked my hair and started kissin' me hard and sloppy. The strong smell of liquor almost made me gag. "Wait! Let me go into the bathroom and freshen up baby." I rubbed his now rock hard dick as he stared at me like he wanted to just chew me like a grilled steak, sautéed in onions, fresh off the flame! "I mean, we have been out all night. I need to wash under my arms and other areas." He slapped my hand away. "Yes, do that. The last thing I need is a funky ass hoe. Hurry up so I can put all this dick on you."

I walked into the bathroom and locked the door behind me. This nigga had another thing comin'! I took my blade out of my purse and tucked it in the back of the one piece lace teddy I wore underneath my dress. I wrapped a towel around my waist in an effort to conceal it. My stockin,'s and shoes were balled up and stuffed inside the dress I wore. When I came out of the bathroom, he was layin' butt naked on top of the covers with his eyes closed. I thought about his nice ass body and how it the sex would have been if he'd just not been a dumb ass educated jerk. As I approached the bed, I dropped my balled up clothes as close to the door as I possibly could. I did a brief observation of the room to see if there was anything that wasn't bolted down, just in case my plan didn't go as I thought it would. I noticed the phone was right next to the bed on the nightstand.

"Come and get this good ass dick!" He spoke with confidence as he stroked his erect penis. I unwrapped the towel and climbed on top of him. Corey grabbed my titties and started bitin' them through my lingerie. I started kissin' his ears and tellin' him how much I wanted him. He tried to penetrate me by slidin' my teddy to the side. That's when I whipped out my blade and stabbed him in his ear. "Bitch! What the fuck?" He grabbed his ear and looked at his hand. By the time he realized he was bleedin', my gut reaction told me to reach for the phone receiver and commit to poundin' him in his face and head with it. So that's what I did. He had delayed reactions thanks to the drinks he guzzled down at the art expo. Whap! Whap! Whap! I just continuously hit him until he lay unconscious bleedin' from the face and ear. I grabbed my clothes off the floor, and the towel on the bed to wrap around myself as I ran out the door fast as hell like a kid behind a ice cream truck.

I called Cassie from a phone booth a couple of blocks away. I was scared and mad as hell! I thought she said she *knew* this nut! She came and picked me up within ten minutes. I cussed her ass o-u-t! From that night on, I would have security in place for my protection. And no more fucked up motels either. If I was gone be escortin' these maniacs to functions, then they would pay the price. It's my choice from now on. I will never be in another fucked up situation; at least not anytime soon.

As I looked myself over in the mirror one last time, my eyes started to water. I was happy with the money I was makin', but deep down inside I knew what I was doin' was wrong. The attitude I had goin' into this life was now not the frame of mind I'd been in for the past few months. What was I doin' to myself? And worst, what would momma and Jeremy do to me if they found out? Momma had taught me all these years that my body was my temple. She said. "A man will only do what you allow him to do."

The first tear fell and so did I. I dropped to the floor and prayed like I never prayed before. "Please God, forgive me my sins; for all that I have done and for what I'm about to do. Bless me and keep my family and me safe." I got up off the floor, wiped my eyes, and grabbed my car keys off the dresser.

When I stepped on the landin' downstairs and headed for the door, momma was sittin' on the couch snappin' peas as she watched her favorite soap operas. She and grandma had been out to the Eastern Market earlier this mornin'. "Where you goin'?" I hesitated like I was all into the t.v. as I searched through my bag of lies database for an answer. "Ummm, I have a date with this guy I met at the bar a couple of weeks ago." I stammered over my words as the lie flowed fluently over my tongue. I hated lyin' to momma but I didn't want her to worry about me any more than she usually did.

Her headaches seemed to be under control thanks to her new blood pressure medication. She'd been diagnosed with hypertension; the fancy medical name for high blood pressure. A few months back, momma scared Jeremy and me shitless! Her nose was bleedin' uncontrollably and she was cryin' and prayin' at the same time. She'd told us that her head was hurtin' worse than it had ever hurt before. Jeremy and I had cold rags on her head, nose and neck. Momma looked like a sick bloody mummy. When the ambulance got there, I rode in the back with her as Jeremy followed behind in the Deuce. The doctors told us that if we hadn't gotten momma there when we did, she probably would have had a stroke. Her blood pressure was so high that it wouldn't give an accurate readin'. They ended up keepin' her for a couple of days for observation.

From that moment on Jeremy and I made changes around the house. I started overseein' the daily routines that momma did like a ritual;makin' sure the house was clean from top to bottom, and washin' momma's and my clothes before sneakin' off to work. Jeremy stepped up to the plate more too. He helped me in the kitchen and washed his own clothes; for a change.

It didn't take much more than the hearin' the word "stroke" used in the same sentence with momma's name for Jeremy and I both to know how much she really meant to us; now more than ever. To have her stressin' about Jeremy and me, or anything for that matter, was now a thing of the past. And I definitely wanted to keep it that way. Jeremy did too, but he seemed to have a botched up way of doin' it.

Momma continued snappin' peas and lookin' at the televison through me. It was as if she felt that somethin' wasn't right with me. Or, am I just paranoid because I know what I'm about to go do? She continued drillin' me. "So, why haven't I met this young man? Does he live around here?"

My heart started beatin' fast. But even so, I continued with the lie I originally started. "I just want to be sure he's straight first momma, before I start invitin' him over for fine wine and cheese! You know we can't just have anybody comin' over here. And besides, I haven't even talked to Jeremy about him yet."

If there was one thing momma knew for sure, it was that anyone I even *thought* about datin' had to have Jeremy's seal of approval first. He wouldn't have it any other way. Jeremy was very particular about the men invited to our home. So far it had only been DeAngelo, Damon, Calvin, Andrew and Mr. Monroe. Everybody else could describe the *outside* of the house to a 'tee'. That's all they would see unless they went to the garage to conduct business with Jeremy. And not many of them were allowed inside the garage.

"Just be careful Berry! It's a lot of crazy people runnin' around this city just waitin' to do dirt." If only she knew I'd actually been with a few of them! "You got your mace?" Momma yelled as I walked out the door. I reached in my purse and pulled out the can that she had given me three months ago! I held it up so she could see I had it. "I'll be alright momma! It's just for a bite to eat and a couple of drinks. I'll try not to come in too late." I blew her a kiss through the screen and got in the car.

SHOES

These are the BEST pair of shoes I have and I'm glad to kick
them off at the end of the day.
All I can say is I'm grateful to have been blessed even with
just this one pair.
Although the souls are worn and the material they're made of
is tattered and torn they still get me from point A to B.

It just trips me out how people see these shoes and judge
them by their appearance;
They don't carry a known designer's name; but these shoes I
wear are NOT the same ones in the store;
They hold MORE than the average person can begin to
imagine.
The shoes I wear explore all unknown destinations to
journeys far beyond reach;
The shoes that teach me to stand upright; they balance me as
I walk paths lit at night.
These shoes I wear keep me firm in my place even if they're
not to the liking of everyone else's taste;
These tattered, torn, nameless shoes will NEVER go to
waste.

And if I take them off....those same people that talked mess
will try to squeeze in just to see why I never chose to throw
them away.
They'll sarcastically say, "Why is she keeping these old busted
pair of shoes?"
My answer will simply be, "because that's what I CHOOSE

D'Aviér

to do!"

Then they'll talk about me as they walk away and start
rumors; all the while my head will STAY
raised and I'll smile......

These shoes are made for me only..... And NONE of you
could EVER even BEGIN to walk my mile!
~D'Aviér

All Work and No Play

When I reached the main entrance of the Double Tree hotel located in Southfield, I noticed that there was a crowd of people standin' in the lobby. The valet attendant came and escorted me out of the car. He was so cute. His boyish appearance reminded of this guy named Omar that I had a crush on years ago. I never told him that I liked him, and I'm glad I didn't. He ended up in prison for molestin' his twelve year old cousin when he was eighteen. Ain't that some shit? He was cute though. "You look nice today!" Ok, I had to ask myself, "Is he tryin' to flirt with me?" It was a cute gesture, but he looked to be about a hot twenty. His green eyes looked hazel from an angle. Never-the-less, he made me blush from ear to ear. "Thank you. You look just as nice in your uniform!" I wasn't sure if I offended him or not because he kinda had a smirk on his face like he wanted to call me a bitch.

He handed me my keys and pointed to the entrance to the lobby. "Have a good day." I tried to be polite because I didn't want to leave on a bad note. You never know who you might need to help you one day. In this line of business, it wasn't wise to make a lot of enemies.

When I walked into the lobby of the hotel I hesitated. This place was beautiful. The ceilings were gold and had angels that lined the trim surroundin' the marbled walls. The front desk was also marble, but the countertop was glass. The carpet was multicolored and blended perfectly with the walls. I'd decided to wait in the lobby for a minute to see if

D'Aviér

this guy would eventually come lookin' for me. This way I could get a sneak peak at the "goodies". I knew firsthand that looks can be deceivin', but maybe I could somehow peep his character too.

I took a seat on the burgundy leather couches located in the center of the lobby. There were magazines lined up on the glass coffee tables in the center of where the couches were arranged. The real trees put the finishin' touches to the lounge area. I grabbed one of the _Time_ magazines and flicked through the pages, occasionally lookin' up at the front desk to see if any men stood around like they were lookin' for somebody. I knew I would recognize him from the picture.

Twelve minutes went by and nothin'! No one had even come to check in come to think of it. Just as I put the magazine on the table and walked towards the front desk to ask for Bryson, there was commotion at the front revolvin' doors.

"Please Mister! I'm begging you! "The pleadin' man had tattered clothes that were filthy and saggin'. His hair was matted and he looked as if he needed to bathe. I stood there for a minute just in case he pulled out a gun or somethin'. I could imagine the reactions on momma's and Jeremy's faces if I got caught up in somethin' at this hotel and if they were to find out what I was really doin' there. So, I laid low just to make sure there were no unfortunate mishaps. "Gone with that mess!" A medium build, stocky guy spoke with his deep voice. He had on a dark blue trench coat and a maroon suit with a gold tie. He resembled the man on the picture that I'd spoken to Cassie about earlier that day. "You can't be comin' around here beggin' for food and scarin' people away. I just gave you forty dollars yesterday man!" The man dropped to his knees right there in the lobby. By now the lobby was startin' to fill with spectators tryin' to get a glimpse of what was goin' on. Hotel security approached the scene in their dark brown uniforms, but they didn't carry guns. "Is everything alright down here?" The first security guard to the scene inquired to make sure the situation was under control. "Please man! I need to lay my head down and take a bath. I promise I won't bother nobody!" Tears seemed to be formin' in the homeless man's eyes, although none actually fell. "What did you do with the money I gave you yesterday man? And get up off the damn floor!"

The homeless man struggled to get to his feet. "I spent the money on food Mr. Bryson. And I bought a blanket and a pillow so I could be comfortable under the overpass. If you don't believe me, here's the receipt." He went into his back pocket and pulled a white piece of paper out. "That could be anybody's receipt! Don't shit me man!" Bryson raised his voice. "You want me to put him out Mr. Bryson? Just say the word and he's out!" The second hotel security officer was all too anxious to throw the guy out. By now I felt sorry for the guy. I mean, just because he was homeless didn't mean he deserved to be treated that way. So, I walked towards the entrance where they were all standin' around. Just as I approached the scene, Bryson came out of his pocket with a "knot." The stack of money was held together by a diamond cut, gold money clip. "Here dog!" He tossed a hundred dollar bill to the young valet as he brought in the rest of Bryson's packages. "Go get this fool a room on your discount and make sure he gets some room service; just for today. And keep the change!" The valet grabbed the money and frowned as he walked to the front desk. It was more irritatin' than the frown he gave me when I complimented him outside. "Thank you Mr. Bryson! I won't let you down, I promise." The homeless man walked to the front desk behind the valet.

"Hello Bryson." I tried to smile as I forced myself to say hello. It wasn't like I wasn't attracted to him. He was fine as hell, but his attitude towards the homeless man made me think he was just another jerk out to show people how powerful he was just because he had money. A lot of guys in the neighborhood were like that once their hustles started to pay off, so I knew this type of arrogance first hand. It was jacked up how he spoke to that man. Momma always said that you never kick a person when they're down. But needless-to-say, I still have a job to do. "And who might you be?" He took my hand and kissed my knuckles. "I'm Berry! We met through Cassie." Although we hadn't actually seen one another, this is the line I would use as a way of disguisin' the profession. "Well it's Berry nice to meet you!" I could hear the two security officers standin' next to him snicker. I hope he didn't think he was he first person to ever use that corny ass line. It was just one of the many I'd heard throughout elementary and junior high school. I just smirked and went with the flow. We went up to the room to discuss the terms of our date. He seemed to be really interested in my likes and interests, but then again, they all seemed that way in the beginnin'. After we chatted for a bit, Bryson left the room only telling me that he needed to take care of something. He told me that he frequented this hotel regularly and that he was very close with security. He said that if I needed anything or if I got hungry while he was gone t I could just call down to the front desk and tell them to put it on his tab. I did just that!

Bryson had been gone for about two hours, which gave me time to set my evenin' wear out and make sure I had my mace and knife tucked away securely in my clutch bag. After I showered and touched up my hair, I sat there bored waitin' for Bryson to come back. I really wanted this date to be over. I really wanted this profession to be over. I grabbed the room service menu off the nightstand and started browsing through it. By the time Bryson came back I was dressed and ready to go. I'd had time to eat and nap and still be dressed and ready to go by 9:30 p.m. "Damn! You look beautiful." I started to be sarcastic; irritated by the two hours I'd been waitin' for him to return. Instead, I said politely, "Thank you for noticin'!" I think my response flew right over his head because he said, "You're welcome. This was the most polite he'd probably been in his entire life. I could care less though. I was just hoping that he didn't find out about that twenty dollar fruit salad I'd ordered and demolished while I waited for him. He must've just missed the bell hop wheelin' the cart out minutes before he returned. I ended up waitin' another thirty to forty-five minutes for him to "freshen up." He didn't even get in the shower! He just washed under his arms and threw on another suit. I hoped he wasn't expectin' anything afterwards. I couldn't help but to think about the homeless man from earlier. How could Bryson talk down to him? At least the homeless man wanted to wash his ass and get out of those dirty ass clothes. Bryson had been gone for hours doin' God knows what, but yet only washed under his arms. I'll bet his balls were screamin' for a shower by now.

On the way out of the room I packed the clothes I changed out of and put them into my overnight bag. Bryson waited as I had the valet show me to my car; I tossed the overnight bag into the trunk. I couldn't explain it, but for some reason I wanted to play sick and get out of this date. I contemplated my reasons in my head as I walked to meet Bryson back at the front where his blue Suburban with the tinted windows was parked. Somethin' just made me feel uneasy about him and escortin' him on this date. But I shook it off and kept rollin'. I took a peek at my pager after I fastened my seat belt. No call from Cassie; not one. I just knew she'd be callin' to make sure that I followed through with the date. It wasn't unusual for her not to call; just odd that she didn't. I convinced myself silently. Maybe she's at the house with Jeremy tryin' to keep him preoccupied until I get off "work." I'm sure he'd asked if she'd seen or talked to me since I wasn't home when he got there.

Bryson tried to make conversation. "So, what made you decide to be an escort? I mean, you look like you come from a good background." He turned the jazz music down so he could hear my response. I couldn't help but to think to myself how he could tell what type of background I came from. I mean, sure Cassie set up the date, but one of our terms of agreement was that she never discuss anything about me. I knew she couldn't have told him who I was because she didn't want to risk Jeremy and my mom findin' out, just like *I* didn't want to risk it. "What makes you think I came from a good background?" I had to know why Bryson made that assumption. I was waitin' for his response to contain Cassie's name. I'm not kiddin'. My heart was pumpin' like I was about to go into cardiac arrest. If this bitch said *anything* about Jeremy bein' my brother! If she even named a street within the vicinity of McKinley, I swear I was gone pounce on her like a hungry ass tiger on a deer. Bryson stammered over his words, "I just mean you look nice. You're pretty and you seem like you're too nice and prissy to be escorting men around town. I can't see a nigga not just swooping you up and making you his woman." Whew! I felt like a weight was lifted off my shoulders. There were times when I questioned Cassies' motives, but for the most part, I took a likin' to her because she was about her business and she always kept it real with me. I knew she wasn't like all the other girls that just wanted to hang around me to find out info about Jeremy. Cassie and I were beyond that. There were times before I even got into this profession that she would come to the house just to kick it with me. A lot of those times Jeremy would be in and out, but she never stopped kickin' it with me to go off somewhere with Jeremy. I was just glad that Bryson didn't say what I thought he would. It felt good knowin' that Cassie could honestly be trusted. He continued with his line of questionin' as we cruised to the location of the event. "Do you have any sisters or brothers?" *Now* he was gettin' personal. "Are you the police?" Cassie taught me to ask that when a client seemed to want to know personal background information. Bryson laughed. "Hell naw. You think I'm a punk ass police?" He was amused with my inquiry. "I'm just sayin'. You're askin' me questions like you need to know possible contact information or somethin'. To answer your question, no. I'm the only child." I lied. I didn't think it was his business. I was only there to escort him and it wasn't like I was about to start datin' his ass. So what did it really matter if I had siblings at home? I guess he could tell that I was bothered by his conversation because he turned up the volume when Kenny G's clarinet played. It didn't bother me one bit. I was relaxed and ready to get this night over with. I even had time to make my getaway excuse. Just in case he wanted "dessert" after our dinner date. Hell, I was already full anyway.

The suburban finally came to a stop. We'd driven from the hotel in Southfield to another place located somewhere in Novi, Michigan. I hadn't really paid much attention to the exit we came off of, but I didn't feel like I was in any danger where I had to take a mental note of the directions we took. Besides, the parkin' lot to this place was packed! There was nothin' but new cars on the lot. Mercedes, Suburban's, BMW's, decked out Thunderbird classics. You name it, it was parked there. There were 3 Bentley's parked alongside the entrance of the establishment. This was definitely a ballers' event. I grabbed my waist length mink trimmed sweater to cover my open arms. It was a little chilly for the beginnin' of July.

When we entered the hall, there were all kinds of suits standin' in the corridor. The men there were definitely dressed for the occasion. Most of them looked like straight up pimps in Dobbs brimmed hats, with their fancy pin-striped suits. Some had mega diamond pinky rings, while others flashed their gold teeth and Gucci link chains with matchin' bracelets. The females weren't holdin' them up either! There was this one female dressed in a blue kimono with the matchin' floor length jacket. The leather straps on her sandals had real diamonds linin' the elastic that held her feet in place. Her hair was up in a French roll and she had those things that look like chop sticks holdin' it in place. That too had diamonds in it. Although I didn't have a lot of them, I was a diamond connoisseur! I knew the real thing. Whoever this lady was, she *had* to be the head bitch in charge. The females standin' around her proved to be humbled in her presence. Bryson motioned for me to come over to the table where he was chit-chattin' with a few of the men in the corridor. He told one of the females behind the champagne filled table our names as she checked the guest list. She wrote our names on name tags, passed them to us to put on, and told us to grab a glass of champagne as the greeter came out to show us to our assigned table. I was completely impressed. I'd been to a lot of events, but this one topped it all. It was so well organized and nobody had to wait in line or anything like that. Bryson extended his arm for me to grab hold of as we were escorted into another part of the hall. This was where the main event would take place. As we entered the room, the banner over the stage read: *Welcome to the 6th Annual Literary Ball.*

I couldn't believe my eyes! The ceiling was painted a metallic light grey and it was trimmed in gold. It wasn't the paint that caught my attention though. There was a beautiful antique looking chandelier centered in the room. It took up basically the middle of the hall. The crystals hangin' from them shined like new diamonds as the soft fluorescent lights gleamed colors of richness through them. The color of the ceilin' made the sparkles seem to bounce around like a disco ball in a club. There were smaller chandeliers placed throughout the rest of the ceilin'; miniature replicas of the *grand* fixture.

The high back chairs were covered in purple suede-like seat covers with a silver bow sachet. The round tables were spaced about 6 inches apart; a total of fifty tables for guests, each seating 6 people. Mixed red flowers filled the tall glass centerpieces. There were circle cut mirrors under the centerpieces, atop the metallic table clothes. It was decorated so eloquently. The purple stage background looked to be the same material of the chair covers and proved to be a royal color.

As I looked around the room I noticed that each seat in the hall had been occupied. And there were still people comin' in! The kitchen staff had to take out 2 more tables for some late stragglers who were more than likely tryin' to be seen. Never-the-less, everyone in attendance was dressed to kill! I felt like I was under dressed. "You straight Berry?" Bryson must have seen the amazement on my face. I stumbled to answer. "Yeah, I'm….I'm straight." Bryson scooted his chair closer and leaned over so that he wouldn't be shoutin' over the various conversations that bounced off the walls throughout the hall. "So, you gone take that jacket off?" He looked down at my perfectly perched breast through my two unbuttoned buttons. "That's the look I was going for," is the thought that crossed my mind. This man was scrumptious. Just lookin' at him made me wanna lick my lips! "I'm gonna take it off Bryson." I said it in a soft voice like we'd been kickin' it for a while. That's just how fine he was, but still….. I wasn't lettin' my guard down. It's the nice pretty boys you gotta watch! They the freakiest ones; want you to do *all* the kinky shit in the world. Don't get me wrong, I was into "mildly kinky." But *sadistic* was not a part of my job description. It wasn't even in the fine print. Since

I'd had this happen to me in past events, I decided to go with my gut instinct. I'd already said I wasn't gone get into any *aerobic sessions* with Bryson. I debated mentally between callin' home and havin' momma page me, or just actin' like I came on my period in the bathroom. I thought to myself, "If I call momma and ask her to call me back, she's gonna worry herself to death in between dialin' the numbers. Then she'll hear the background and get to askin' me a *trillion* questions. Auntie "Flow" it is! I mean, what's he gonna do? I know he ain't gone ask me to see! Then again…..with some niggaz, you never know."

Just as I stepped out of my thought, Bryson was standin' there talkin' to an associate. He was a skinny dude with a peach three piece suit that went perfectly with his peach 'big block' gators. He had on a cream brimmed hat that donned a peach ribbon around it. His dollar sign cufflinks added the finishin' touches to his "polished" look. The feather in his hat didn't go though. I chuckled to myself!

He wanted to look so 'fly' that he went and plucked a damn feather from what looked like it could have once belonged to a goose. The tip of the feather was bent up and it looked disheveled. Like the bird was probably caught off guard or somethin'. Other than the feather, brother looked nice. I chuckled again anticipatin' which direction the feather would be in once the drinks started flowin'!

As Bryson exchanged compliments with other guys comin' up to the table, I continued to glance around the room in search of possible familiar faces. I wasn't tryin' to have no surprises tonight. For some reason I wasn't worried about anybody dry snitchin' about me bein' at the event, but just the fact of bumpin' into somebody that may know me or my family gave me chills. You could tell it was orchestrated by people who shared a common interest because the majority in attendance was either escorts, entrepreneurs; commonly referred to as pimps, women on their payroll, and the people they knew that lived the same lifestyle. This place was definitely above the McDaniel family budget.

As people found their way to the seats of their choice, the waiters dressed in black slacks and white shirts served Champaign and white wine to each table. The stage lights began to brighten. The sound crew checked the speakers and microphones one last time before all in attendance were called to order. I decided to take a trip to the restroom to freshen up my make-up. As I made my way past the table placed right before the hallway entrance to where the "dolls" room was located, I noticed a familiar face. It was some guy that had on a tan suit. He was facin' towards the female he was talkin' to, but I wasn't sure if it was somebody I'd seen since we'd been seated. "Oh, well," I thought. He was probably an old client. I just hoped it wasn't the one that I had to cut!

There was a line by the rest room, but no one in the line waitin' for a stall. These were females that knew each other at some point in life… or not. Every one of them stood there like they were waitin' for the photographers to come in at any given minute. They acted like they were there for a photo shoot for a spot on the cover of *Essence* magazine. Some were definitely paired up with their own renditions of a black Hugh Heffner; ready and willin' to strip down to their bare ashy ass ankles for the highest bidder. Although the majority of them seemed to be classy, there were a hand full of them that rose through the ranks from hoein' on the streets to being wined and dined in luxurious hotel suites. Their "hood-ish" ways took over when they talked.

"Excuse me?" A voice behind me was tryin' to get somebody's attention. "Hey girl!" I turned around with an irritated look on my face. I didn't know who she was talkin' to, but I was dyin' to see who would respond to her ignorant ass "Hey Girl" call. "You; over there with the mink!" The girls standin' around her started snickerin'. I looked around to see who the fuck she was talkin' to and who her audience was laughin' at. Luckily for them, a female behind me answered, "What the hell you callin' me fo?" They all started laughin' as she walked over toward the "clique." All I could think was, "I *knew* that bitch wasn't talkin' to me! 'Ol Ghetto ass." My tolerance level for females was at an all-time low. There was too much competition in this line of business than to be tryin' to make friends. I was one of the lucky ones because I worked independently under Cassie and there wasn't a whole crew of us waitin' for our assignments to be passed out. Plus, if I didn't feel like participatin' I had a *voice* in the matter. "Hoes" didn't have that option with their pimps. Cassie was showin' me a means of makin' my own money. She never once profited from my gain. Then again, actually she did. She knew that I could tell Jeremy about it. All I had to do was flip the script and make him believe that she *forced* me into it. That would be the end of Cassie and Jeremy. But, she made my brother happy and helped me make money in the process. I guess I'll let her stay around; for Jeremy's sake if nothin' else. That's the one major thing she and I had in common; love for my brother.

I turned back around and reached for the big half circle knob leadin' to the lounge area in the restroom. Same story in here! Females in front of the mirror like they about to shoot their next actin' scene. I saw more tuckin', pullin', and brushin' of weave than I saw in the high school locker room after gym class. These women thought they were the baddest things on earth since the creation of Barbie. I have to give it to some of them though. Their make-up was laid and they had stomachs that were as flat as a white girl's ass! Talk about dressed! They looked like they were "top shelf." Of course a lot of them were snooty. The look-you-up-and-down and then *still* won't speak to yo' ass type females. I wasn't pressed though 'cuz I looked equally as good. My shit cost just as much as theirs.   And although I didn't wear much jewelry, the shit I had on made that much of a difference. Nothin' gaudy; just simple with lots of bling! My tennis bracelet was two carats by itself.   My earrings equivalent, and to top it off I had a rectangular, slightly raised ROCK on my middle right hand finger that was encircled by pure mother of pearl. 4 carats total! So what if it had been on three separate lay-a-way plans. It was paid for, and it was mines. Once I came out of the stalls I approached the mirrors over the black granite counters. I looked up and noticed a woman comin' out of the stall next to mines. My eyes got big as watermelons when I finally realized who she was. I did a double take just to be absolutely sure of the face.   Sure enough, it was exactly who I thought it was!   It was Ms. Beldon; DeAngelo's grandmother!

Before I could hold my head down and act like I hadn't noticed her, she'd seen my reflection through the mirror. "Berry?" She squinted her eyes like she was unsure. I acted like I was shocked, "Ms. Beldon?" She laid her cane with the fancy handle up against the sink and gave me a big hug! It kind of caught me off guard because last I remembered; Ms. Beldon was *not* a friendly woman. Hell, she didn't even speak to me at DeAngelo's funeral. But then considerin' the circumstances, I guess she wasn't in the mood for much conversation at that time. "How have you been?" She checked me over from head to toe tryin' not to be obvious. "I'm fine Ms. Beldon. We hadn't seen you in such a long time we thought you'd moved outta state." Angelo's grandmother smiled as she washed her hands. "Naw baby. I ain't move outta town, I just went away for a minute. I had some things I needed to take care of after....... I cut her off, "Jeremy said he wanted to know where you were so he could make sure you were alright." I talked to her through the mirror as I put my hair up with the fancy butterfly clip that grandma had given me years ago.

Ms. Beldon changed the subject. "How *is* Jeremy?" She said it as if she knew something or heard something. "He's fine. You know Jeremy Ms. Beldon; *still* bein' Jeremy and gettin' on me and momma's nerves!" I fake laughed. "Is that right?" Ms. Beldon dried her hands and threw away the tissue she'd used. "So, your momma been alright? How's her headaches?" Ok, now this question really caught me off guard. I knew I'd never discussed momma's headaches with anyone outside the family. And to my knowledge, Jeremy didn't either. We were very committed to keepin' our family business *in the family*. Maybe Jeremy mentioned it to DeAngelo? I know that sistah Beulah knew, cuz she'd been at our house a couple of times when momma had episodes.

But sistah Beulah and Ms. Beldon didn't talk if my memory serves me right.... Or did they? "They're fine and under control. She hasn't had one in a long time now." I lied. Momma had been hospitalized due to those damn migraines. But, I wasn't at ease discussin' momma's health with Ms. Beldon. Even though I cared for Angelo, I wasn't comfortable talkin' to Ms. Beldon in depth about my family. I figured anything that she already knew about us had to come from DeAngelo *before* he died. As far as I was concerned, that was all the information she needed to know. "Well, it was good seeing you Berry, wit' yo' pretty self! My grandson know he liked him some Berry!" My eyes started tryin' to water as I smiled from ear to ear. I never knew that DeAngelo told anyone that he liked me; let alone his grandmother. "Yeah, he adored you and Jeremy. You be careful out here." Ms. Beldon gave me one last hug and reached to go out of the door. Then she paused and turned towards me as she reached in her clutch purse. "If you need anything Berry, make sure you give me a call. Maybe call me so we can have Sunday dinner or something." I grabbed the card from the hand she extended to me. "I would like that very much Ms. Beldon. Thanks for the invitation." She walked out of the bathroom with two other females followin' behind her. Before I put the card in my purse, I checked myself over again one last time. I was puzzled as to why Ms. Beldon hadn't questioned what I was doin' at this event. Of all her line of questionin', never once did she inquire as to who I was with or anything relatin' to my presence at this place. Then I thought to myself, "Hell, what is *she* doin' here?" I looked down at her card that read:

Queen Bee's Escort Services Inc.
Providing Quality Dating Srvcs. for Quality Men
Divine Beldon Esq.

I couldn't believe my eyes. "This is DeAngelos' *grandmother*," is all I could think to myself. So, all the "rumors" about her puttin' her grandson up on the game *had* to be true. That's why she didn't ask me what I was doin' there......she already knew! There was no way that she couldn't have known; especially since she gave me her card. I tucked the card in my purse and proceeded out the door.

The line in the hallway had cleared out. Of course there were other's out in the hallway talkin' about the people they worked for and all the material items they had. I laughed to myself, "Not only hoes, but materialistic hoes on top of that." Then I frowned. How could I talk about them? *I'm amongst my peers!* The thought irritated me as I made my way back to my seat. As I walked back to the area where Bryson and I were seated, I took a quick glimpse to see if I could see where Ms. Beldon, or should I say "Divine", was seated. The lights had been dimmed and the stereo speakers were filled with soft classical music as the event coordinators made last minute preparations before startin'.

"Damn! I thought I was gone have to send somebody to come get you!" Bryson acted like he missed me while I was gone. His deep dimples pierced through his neatly trimmed cheeks as he smiled at me. His goatee was fully shaded and trimmed up so perfect. The smell of his *Jovan's Sex Appeal* cologne proved to tell a story about his appearance. "So, are you sayin' you missed me?" I seductively picked up my flute of wine and took a squig; tryin' my best to keep up this charade. "Yeah, I missed you. But, I'm sure we'll make up for it tonight." Bryson grabbed my left hand and gave it a squeeze. Hated to disappoint his sexy, itch balls ass, but it was not goin' down like that! I didn't even come out with my lie yet 'cuz then he may have suspected somethin'. So, I just went with the flow. I'd break the news to him after the show. Plus, I was tryin' to get myeat on. You could smell greens and chicken cookin' in the back. That's one thing about black folk! We attend some of the fanciest parties and will dress our asses off, but no matter what the occasion is nor where it's located; soul food goes with every thang! I planned on eatin' like it was Jesus servin' the Last Supper!

"Testing....Testing." The m/c for the night talked over the elevator music. "Ladies and gentlemen, may I have your attention please? Before we get started, we'd like to make sure that everyone interested in participating has turned in their poetry to Lady *FeNique*. Raise yo' hand woman so the people can see you." Laughter erupted from various tables. "There she is over there by the bar.....her favorite place!" People began laughin' at his corny ass jokes like he was a real stand-up comedian or somebody. Maybe after I had a few more glasses of wine he'd be funny to me too. I waved to the waiter standin' a couple of tables over. Once I got his attention, I held my glass up motionin' for a refill. "Can you just bring me a bottle"? Bryson whipped out a stack of money. I guess he called himself flossin' or something, but I wasn't a bit impressed. I knew he thought he was gone get somethin' tonight and I wasn't even tyrin' to entertain the thought. The waiter, on the other hand, must've really been excited by Brysons' stash, 'cuz all I saw was the back of his coat as he practically ran to the kitchen. He was goin' so fast he damn near tripped a couple of people along the way.

"You know you didn't have to do that Bryson." Bryson smiled, showin' his front pearly whites. "Do what? I mean, it ain't *nothin'* to me. You enjoy drinking wine and I enjoy watchin' you drink it! What sense does it make to keep callin' penguin boy over here to get you a refill when you could just have the bottle in front of you and pour as much as you want, whenever you want?" Ok, I had to admit he was right, BUT….. I knew this nigga was tryin' to get me drunk. Just as the waiter returned to the table, Bryson's pager went off. He looked down at it as if he was irritated by the digits displayed. "What *this* nigga want?" Bryson talked aloud as he got up from the table. "I'll be right back Berry. I gotta make this call right quick." I never said a word. I could care less about him leavin' the table. I just wasn't feelin' him like that; cute or not. I poured another glass of wine; my second so far, waitin' for the main event. As long as I had my mace and blade in my clutch purse and my money tucked in my bra, I was straight. I didn't have a thing to worry about.

"Yeah, this is Bryson." Bryson had gone outside to use his cell phone in his car. "She's here with me. She's waitin' on me to come back in." The voice on the line seemed to irritate him. "She wasn't at the room long enough for me to take it. Hell, by the time I got back in there from Delaney's room takin' her picture, Berry was already dressed." Bryson explained himself to the inquiries comin' through the receiver. "Listen Man! You ain't got to be hollerin' at me like that!" Irritated by the male tone on the opposite line, Bryson took a deep sigh. He looked himself over in the mirror above

D'Aviér

the visor in his Suburban. Reachin' in his glove box, he pulled out his bottle of *Sex Appeal* out and touched up his clothes as he continued his conversation. "Ok. I'll take her straight back to the room and work on that. I just hope Delaney don't get suspicious." "Damn Delaney!" The voice on the other line came through Bryson's receiver. "Listen man! I know I owe you; BE-LI-EVE me I do. You won't ever let me forget." Bryson was being sarcastic. "I'm gone take care of Berry just like I did Delaney. After this we should be even and I'm done Calvin. I mean, I been workin' this debt off for three years now man. I got enough in my pocket to cover the interest." Bryson prepared to exit the SUV. "Yeah, I'll call you once she goes to change clothes. I'll let the phone ring once and then hang up. I'll call you back when I have the picture in my hand." Bryson hung up the phone and cut the ignition off. He mumbled under his breath, "I'll be glad when this shit is over. This nigga done got on my *last* nerve!" He headed back towards the entrance of the hall.

My Undivided Attention

By the time Bryson reappeared at the table, I'd heard three poems and drank four glasses of wine. I knew I had to slow down when I ended up with the hiccups. The "poets" told stories about their lives through their rhymin' flows. The first person was a guy dressed like a straight up pimp. Ok, the majority of them were dressed up and looked good, but this one was a pimp from waaaay back in the day! Like a 1965 pimp; the one's that used to be in them old movies momma would watch with that actress lady, Pam Grier. He walked up on that stage with those Bootsy Collins and the Funkadelics silvery gray platform boots on with the matchin' cape! He spoke all slow and was rhymin' his words; just like them ol' school characters. The name of his six line poem was: *Only My Hoes Know.* I almost laughed so damn hard that I would have spit wine all over myself and the lady sittin' next to me with the silver sequenced dress. She REALLY thought she was a super star. Remember how I told you that the light from the crystals bounced off the walls? Well, after they bounced off the walls it would occasionally bounce off her dress. Some friendly ass lady at the table just had to make mention of it like it was so important for her to know; such *vital* information. Well, the dress was pretty and the light did look attractive the way it cascaded around the sequence, but her ugly ass attitude and face made a perfect pair. This bitch didn't even acknowledge the comment from the lady in the orange silk dress. Her snobbish ass didn't even give her eye contact. Her man must've definitely had her in check 'cuz she sat quietly, eyes forward, mouth closed. "Better her than me", I thought to myself.

The second person recitin' was a female name *D'Aviér* (Dee- ah-vee-ay). She must have lived a hard life because in her poetry she spoke of black holes pullin' her in at a young age and mental demons possessin' every thought she had about the precious gift of life we were all given. It was sweet how she rhymed with her words though. Her vocabulary was extended but not too much that a person would need a Webster on hand in order to relate. I started feelin' her pain towards the end of the poem. I don't know if it was the wine or the vibe I got from her spoken words, but my eyes started to water. She *definitely* spilled her heart *and* soul out on that stage. The way she recited made me look at poetry a whole different way. Hell, she made me wanna write poetry!

"What did I miss?" Bryson came back in smellin' good from his twenty five minute phone call. "Damn he looks good!" I thought to myself as I replied, "Nothin' really but Pimp of the year!" I discreetly pointed in the direction of the table where the 'ol school guy with the cape and the "slump" waves. Bryson cracked up! He leaned in to me and told me the "caped avenger's" nickname was Mr. Bot. Now I was laughin' my ass off. I thought about what he had on and just burst out in laughter. Bryson was lookin' at me like he missed the joke. "With that silver cape and those shiny ass boots, I just assumed they called him that because he looked like a ro-bot!" That was the first thing that came to my mind. When I shared that thought with Bryson, he started laughin' out loud. His dimples deepened with his slanted smile. "Naw silly!" Not Bot as in robot, but B-O-T like the letters mean something." I knew the word Bryson was lookin' for was 'acronym' when he tried to explain what he meant but I didn't bother correctin' him. Hell, the way I frequently used improper grammar and slang, he probably didn't think I was smart enough to know what an acronym was. I thought to myself, "I hope this nigga don't think I'm dumb!" I just *had* to let him know I knew what he meant. "Oh, you mean B-O-T like an acronym?" Bryson agreed. "Yeah! That's the word I was looking for." A mental sigh of relief came over me. I was glad it was him that either couldn't remember the word or that didn't know it altogether. "Back in the day, he actually was pimp of the year; although the title was self-proclaimed," Bryson explained. Bot had all the hoes on 10th Street on his 'line'. He used to talk that pimp talk and when other pimps from neighborin' hoods would see him they would crack this joke. The name just ended up stickin' and that's when people first started callin' him "Bot". Then, when the younger cats grew up and modernized the game, he earned the respect and title of *Mr.* Bot." Bryson still failed to tell me what the acronym actually stood for. Of course I had to ask. "So, what was the joke they would crack on him and what does B-O-T really stand for?" Bryson finished the story after he downed a whole glass of wine and poured another. "It wasn't per say a joke, but more like a theme song. All of them used to go to this one shop and get them finger waves. When "Bot" walked in, one of the pimps made this rhyme like: "Man, after you came around I was wonderin' where all my hoes went. From now on yo' name is BOT, 'cuz you got all *my* bitches down on tenth!" Bryson laughed as I sat there blank faced. "Get it? B-O-T; Bitches On Tenth!"

We both laughed and took a sip of champagne. There

was a brief intermission because one of the microphones shorted out as the not-so-funny m/c attempted to introduce the next poet. "I'm gonna go to the ladies room to powder my nose Bryson." I'd always wanted to say that! "Powder my nose!" It sounded so classy in the movies. Come to think of it, it was usually classy people actin' in the movies that often used the phrase. Although, I never quite understood *why* the phrase was used; just sayin' the word "restroom" was enough to let people know what you were gonna do once you got in there. I mean really, was the person that created the phrase thinkin' they were throwin' people off by announcin' they would be in there "powdering" their noses? Well, one thing was for sure; I had to pee and sittin' here ponderin' on where the sayin' came from didn't interest my bladder one bit! "I'll be waiting for you, sexy." Bryson smiled that glamorous smile. His teeth sparklin' white. He looked like a big 'ol glazed honeybun just waitin' to be consumed. But, NOPE! I just wasn't feelin' his chemistry. Plus, I can't seem to shake the thought of him ONLY washin' up under his arms and puttin' on five hundred dollars' worth of clothes; shoes included. The jewelry he had on had to ring his total wardrobe up to fifteen hundred tops. All that money on a funky, yet nicely fit body. He was gone all that time and only tapped a trace of water under his arms.

I graciously walked toward the bathroom area, trying to squeeze my thighs together as discreetly as possible. If somebody was to bump into me, this would turn out to be my most embarrassin' moment. So, I maintained my composure and tried to think of somethin' else to take my mind off of my bladder. It didn't work though. Once I walked past the champagne fountain I fastened my pace. Just when I got to the door I heard somebody call my name. "Berry!" The voice sounded familiar to me so I turned to respond. It was Ms. Beldon walkin' briskly towards me. "I need to talk to you honey." She held the door for me as I ran to the first available stall. "Wooo! Sorry Ms. Beldon, I couldn't hold it!" A sense of relief took over as I drained my overflowin' bladder. When I cleaned up and walked to the sink, Ms. Beldon was checkin' under stall doors to see if anyone was in them. "I need y'all to step out. "Come here Berry." I was shocked that Ms. Beldon wanted to talk to me. I mean, over the years when she attended our church, she never was much of a conversationalist with the other members of the church.   She wasn't even friendly with momma, and her grandson was *always* at our house before he passed.   I'd always wondered if there was some deep down resentment she'd had towards us since Angelo was murdered in our yard.   Everybody knew that momma was the neighborhood "mother"; the overseer of anybody's kid visitin' our house, but just the fact that momma seemed to turn a blind eye to Jeremy's extracurricular activities, it just made me wonder if Ms. Beldon somehow felt that DeAngelo would still be alive if he'd never been at my party that night. It was a thought that I often pondered over myself.   After DeAngelo's death I wished the party never happened. But the truth is, had he not been at the party, he would have probably been dead anyway. Momma always told Jeremy and me, "if you live by the sword, you are *bound* to die by it," That's why she worried so much about Jeremy and the type of people he dealt with.

  "Yes Ms. Beldon?" I tried to mask the anxiety in my

voice. Although we both were in the game, I was still embarrassed that Ms. Beldon knew about my secret life. "Call me Divine baby. Nobody here besides you know me as Ms. Beldon o.k.?" She leaned against the sink as she spoke to me in a motherly tone. "I noticed you're here with Bryson. How long have you been knowing him?" Divine's curiosity made me a little uneasy. "Umm, not long; I mean I was set up to escort him to this event." I didn't want to give her too much information because I wanted to know where her line of questionin' was goin'; for the second time tonight. She looked surprised when I told her that my date with Bryson was arranged. "Oh? So you *work* for somebody?" I wanted to ask her "why?" but I didn't want to come off as rude or disrespectful. That would be a surefire way of having her spread my business. Plus, by the way people were reacting around her; I knew she had clout up in here. I didn't want to do or say anything that might piss her off. Hell, I may need her help with some connections one day. I kept thinkin' to myself that she could be the one to help me get out of this shit. I pulled my compact outta my purse and my mace rolled in the sink. I tried to hurry up and grab it before she saw it. "Well, kind of," I replied. "I have a partner that sets up the dates for me." Divine leaned over next to me. "Well, I'm not tryin' to be in your business sweetheart, but you gotta have a lot of heart to be in this game Berry. This can be a dangerous line of work if you don't watch your back and protect yourself." She looked at me through the mirror; her eyes filled with concern. I was familiar with the look. It's the same look momma gives me when I'm gettin' ready to leave the house. She always has that look when she's worried about Jeremy and me. "I got my mace in my purse Ms. Bel.... I mean "Divine." I knew she'd seen it when I scooped it out of the sink! After all, she was standin' right next to me. "Baby, sometimes a can of mace just isn't enough. I don't know who your contact is, but Bryson is not the one you should be fucking with Berry!" She had my undivided attention. I turned to her and just listened from that moment on. "Baby, Bryson works for one of the dirtiest nigga's I've ever seen. You know who I'm talking about too!" Now I was at a loss for words. Who was she talkin' about and why did she assume that I knew this person? I mean, I was completely dumbfounded. "I don't have time to get into the story right now, but I'll tell you this: after this affair is over make sure you go straight home Berry, ya hear me?" I shook my puzzled head in agreement. "Call me after five tomorrow evening. You still got my card?" I opened my purse to make sure it was still there. "Yea, I got it right here." Just as I was closin' my purse, the lady in the blue kimono came into the bathroom. She pushed the doors opened with force like she thought maybe somebody had placed somethin' in front of them so nobody could get in. "Everything alright Divine?" She looked over at Divine with an irritated look on her face. "Sure it is Madame. Why wouldn't it be?" Ok, I thought Divine was the one with the clout, but by the way she bowed down to this lady, I wasn't so sure anymore. "Madame" as they called her, was THE head female. She just flat out checked Divine as if Divine worked for her. As Divine walked out the door I followed about three steps behind her. "I'm sorry, have we met?" Madame spoke pleasantly and extended her hand to me. "How are you? I'm Madame." I reached to shake her soft, well-manicured hand. "Nice to meet you; and your name is?" I almost felt as if she'd already known my name for some reason. "Berry," I sternly responded. I wanted her to know that I wasn't about to let her punk me the way she did Divine. So, I spoke with authority in my voice when I told her my name. "Nice to meet you Berry. You're here with Bryson aren't you?" Now I was certain she'd known about me before we were formally introduced. Sure, she could have seen me walk in with him, but I just had this feelin' that that wasn't the case. I can't explain it, but I knew I was right on the money. "Yes, I'm accompanying Bryson tonight." I spoke intelligently as I stood upright. "Well, I hope you're enjoying the show. Bryson is a real gentleman, so I'm sure you'll have a great time! If you need anything let me know and I'll make sure you're taken care of." Now I was confused. Not just five minutes ago, Divine stood here and told me to watch out for Bryson and to go straight home. Now, here Madame is tellin' me how much of a gentleman Bryson is! I just said, "O.K, will do" and proceeded out of the restroom. "Oh Berry?" Madame yelled out as half my body was in the hallway. I turned back to look in her direction. "I'm the lady of the evening. If anyone here gives you a problem, point them out to me and they will be dealt with! That goes for male or female." She had a straight face and her tone went "hood." I thought to myself, "Damn! She got it like that?" I just turned away and walked back to the ceremony. "What the fuck is goin' on?" I mumbled under my breath. It wasn't like I could call anybody and get answers to my questions. As far as I knew, Cassie had never been to one of these affairs. She was just forced to sleep with guys for money at a young age; or so she said. I need answers though. I was definitely gone give Divine a call tomorrow.

But for now, I'll catch the rest of the show and plan my escape from Bryson. I'd had my suspicions about him from the get go; now I was really leery. The way I see it, who better to believe about Bryson's character than Ms. Belden... I mean Divine? She's known me since I was a kid. What would she have to gain or lose by forewarnin' me about Bryson? Madame on the other hand had never seen me before a day in her life. But apparently she'd known Bryson for a while due to their line of business. Then again, the same would be true about Divine. I was so confused that my head started hurting. The wine & champagne could have played a factor in it too, so I decided lay off the drinks for the rest of the night. It's time for me to pay close attention to the key players of this event. I needed to be sober and on guard for the rest of the night, just in case.

Once I got back to the table, Bryson was over minglin' with some other chick about four tables over. Luckily he was of no interest to me because the way she was pullin' on him and rubbin' his face and shit, it would have been a serious problem. I was never the jealous type but, like my momma, I've always demanded my respect. Even if she didn't know *who* I was, she damn sure saw us come in here *together*. I was greeted at the table by, of all people, BOT! "Lem'me get that chair for you beautiful." He slid my chair out and pushed me gently until my legs were rested under the table. I acknowledged his courteousness by sayin', "thank you." Unfortunately, "thanks" wasn't enough for him. The next thing I knew, he was slidin' out a chair to sit his tin man lookin' ass in! BOT sat right next to me. I thought to myself,

"Let the games begin!" I may not have been to one of these events before, but I knew enough to know that pimps is always lookin' for hoes! Although I didn't classify myself as anything other than an "escort," to a pimp, it's all the same. "So sweetheart; you into aerobics? 'Cuz I can make you flexible as hell!" He was all in my face with that stank ass cigar breath tryin' to recruit me.   "Naw, I'm into makin' money; *all on my own*!" I attempted to cut at the chase and just be flat out with him so it wouldn't be any misunderstandin'. "Oooo Weee! I like the way you talkin' suga! With a bitch like you on my team we can make mega greens; like a mass makin', ass shakin' money machine. You know what I mean?" Ok, now I'm trippin' cuz I really thought that pimps only rhymed their words on movies or documentaries. But this shit is really happenin' in front of my very eyes! And he said it fast as hell. "Whoeva you down with ain't a *real* pimp. When BOT is around all them otha niggas is exempt; ya dig?" I wanted to laugh out loud so bad. The shit was funny as hell. Especially with that silver ass cape and them platform shoes he had to match it! But, I maintained my composure before I got myself into somethin' for runnin' my mouth. "I don't have a pimp, I work independently," I replied.   "U ain't got no pimp? He sounded surprised. "Then let me put you on *my* line and you can work flex time. You can keep thirty percent and then the rest is mine. I'll provide the minks and all lavish trips and if you a good bitch, I'll even buy you a matchin' Cadillac whip!" By now I'd had enough of this Dr. Seuss rhymin' ass nigga; promisin' me green eggs and ham! Just as I was about to spit my rebuttal rhyme tellin' him to get the fuck out my face because I had a can of mace that would leave his ass blind while I escaped without a trace, Bryson came back to the table. "You miss me baby?" I think Bryson was buzzed up on the wine as he talked to me like we'd been in a relationship for a while. But the truth was, I was glad as hell to see him back at the table just in time to rescue me from "Metallic Pimp." He reached for the wine bottle and swooshed it around to see how much was left. "It's a pleasure to have you join me again!" I replied sarcastically to make him feel as if I really cared that he was over there kickin' it with the female across the room. "Man, dat's one fiesty ass bitch you got sittin' there. She's kinda cute too!" Bot was gettin' up from the table as Bryson was about to sit down. "Mr. Pimp of the Year!" Bryson gave Bot a firm hand smack and a hug as he congratulated him on his achievement. "Berry, this is Bot, the one we talked about earlier." My face automatically frowned up. "We've met," I said irritably through my teeth. "Yeah man, when you done playin' pussy with her, toss that bone over to me!" Ok, now I'd had enough of this wanna be a "g" ass nigga's fucked up comments towards me. I may get paid for escortin' niggas around, but I was NOT a hoe! I do what I do because I WANT to; not because I HAVE to, and I'll be damned if I let this ol' ass man belittle me right to my face. Just as I stood with my purse propped open and my hand on the handle about to check this nigga, Bryson put his hand on my shoulder as if to say, "I got this!" He still had the bottle with a corner of wine in his hand. "Ok Bot. That's enough man. She ain't like the other bitches in here. She ain't on the corners man, so show her a little respect." When Bryson said that, I noticed the other ladies at the table turn and start lookin' at me. At first I was mad 'cuz that shit sounded like a

D'Aviér

semi-half ass compliment slash insult. But, I shortly realized that it fucked them up that Bryson was standin' up for me and I wasn't a "*regular.*" The snoody bitch at the table with the sequenced dress on frowned at me and rolled her eyes. "Oh?Alright; my bad "Brice." Excuuuuse me! I didn't realize she was a *high* priced hoe! Forgive my pimp-a-liscious oversight! Hee,hee,hee." Before I knew it, Bryson had done picked the bottle up off the table about to bust Bot in the head! Just as he swung it to hit Bot, I grabbed his arm. "Forget it Bryson, he ain't worth it!" Everybody at our table was now standin' up and clearin' the way for what they thought would be an altercation. "She ain't worth it either Bryson! Put the bottle down, he drunk. You know how Bot get when he get drunk." The bitch with the glitter back dress was talkin' to Bryson…about me! Now, I may not wanna put myself in a man's position, although I was prepared to, but it wasn't a bitch in the world besides my grandma and momma that I wouldn't step to! "What da fuck you talkin 'bout bitch? Sit yo ass down and shut da fuck up! I done told yo 'bout running yo' mouth and getting' in folks business, didn't I? You wanna talk about something; explain why yo' ass was fifty dollars short the last 2 nights? Hunh?" SMACK! Her pimp interjected and then smacked the shit outta her ass; right then and there! I guess that fifty dollars had been on his mind during the whole show! Now all eyes was focused on her! She was lookin' so dumb. At first I kind of felt sorry for her, but then after about two seconds, I realized that she fuckin' deserved it for bein' all up in *my business.* Not only was the light bouncin' off her dress, but now it was shinin' on that big ass hand print on the left side of her face too! "Oh nigga! You wanna be pickin' up bottles and shit?" Bot was still talkin' shit amongst the confusion. Bryson placed the wine bottle down on the table and straightened out his suit jacket. "Man, I ain't even about to go there with yo' drunk ass! Get your stuff Berry so we can get outta here." I couldn't have agreed more that it was time for us to go. All this time I was worried about drawin' attention to myself just to have somebody else do it for me! I grabbed my clutch off the table and headed towards the door with Bryson. At this point, my buzz from the wine had completely diminished. I was more than ready to end this night.

Just as Bryson and I headed towards the hallway leadin' to the exit, somebody yelled his name. "Bryson! It ain't over yet nigga! Yo' head will be on a platter when "Cal" hears this shit! You ain't no pimp nigga! You a broke ass flunkie. Remember this night!" It was Bot yellin' down the hall. His drunken voice bounced off the walls. Bryson didn't bother respondin' to the threat imposed on him. He grabbed my arm and led me to the front exit. "Later for this shit man!" Bryson mumbled under his breath. We jumped into his truck and rode off.

The Long Ride Home

Bryson didn't even bother playin' any music on our way back to the hotel. I wanted to thank him for stickin' up for me, but I didn't want to bring up the altercation. So, I decided to just wait for him to say something first. "You hungry Berry?" Bryson didn't even bother lookin' my way as he inquired about my appetite. He still had that serious look on his face from when we left the hall. "Yeah, I guess." I downplayed the fact that I was starvin'! I hadn't eaten since the evenin' began when I ordered all that fruit at the hotel. Now I was ready for some meat and potatoes. My stomach was hollerin' at me to feed it! "What do you have in mind?" Although he didn't say whether he had an appetite or not, I figured he'd had an idea of a restaurant along the way. "I know this little place on the east side that sells steaks by the pound. It's a hole-in-the wall, but the food is good as hell!"

We pulled up into the parkin' lot of the little restaurant that sat on the corner of Gratiot & Chalmers. Bryson got frustrated because the lot only held about eight spaces, and none seemed big enough to accommodate his truck. "Damn! This little ass parking lot. All the money these nigga's makin' you would think they'd buy the business next door and expand." He was right. But even if they did do that, it would only be a lot full of occupied spaces filled with people sittin' in their cars waitin' to get a spot in this joint. It sat singled off from any other buildin' and it was small as hell. Bryson opened the door to *Capers* and I walked in before him. WOW! The place was little, but it was set up real nice. There was an area where you had to walk up a couple of stairs that served as like a balcony and the bar was towards the back of the room. There were tables off to the right of the entrance that sat in front of mirrored walls. Tables were on the left and right as you got closer to the bar and there was red carpet on the floors that blended perfectly with the wooden stained panelin' on the walls. Al Green screamed out of the speakers, "Love will make you do wrong, yeah!" The chorus faded in the background singin', "Love & Happi-ness." This place was the prime example of why we shouldn't judge a book by its cover. To see it on the outside, you wouldn't have stopped if you were ridin' past and didn't already know about it. But the inside was soulful and offered a relaxin' environment. "How many with you tonight?" The waitress came over with menus in her hand. "Two; non-smoking." Bryson answered and followed behind the waitress. I was wonderin' where she was gone seat us 'cuz this place was packed! She led us up the four steps to a cozy little section in the back. "This is the only table we have right now, sorry!" Bryson turned and looked back at me. I guess that was my queue to give my seal of approval. "It's perfect", I replied.

As Bryson pushed my chair in I said, "I thought you said this place was just a whole in the wall?" "It is!" Bryson answered as he put his suit jacket behind his chair. "I mean, for a young woman like you, you're probably used to eating in top notch restaurants." I smiled at the compliment. Actually he was right though! Mc Donald's and Burger King was a no no from the beginnin' of my life. I'd been eatin' from "Mom's Top Notch Kitchen" all my life! Good ass home cooked meals. Fast food would have went out of business if momma had her own restaurant.

I looked around as one of the waitresses brought plates to the party sittin' in front of us. Daaaaamn! The steak she had on this plate was literally hangin' off the sides of the plate! It was thick as hell and the aroma made my mouth water. I thought slob was gonna run out the side of my mouth. She had another waitress help her deliver the remainin' items for the party of four. Somebody at the table ordered a loaded baked potato garnished with creamy cheese, broccoli spears and bacon bits. That potato was just as big as the steak that sat next to it! Ok, now I know my cuteness and etiquette was about to fly right out the window. Fuck a salad and endless breadsticks, I'm about to get my g-r-u-b on! "Damn that steak is big!" Bryson yelled across the room to one of the guys in the party of four. "Hell yeah man! And not a bite of it is gonna be left!" The guy replied to Bryson as he cut through the medium well steak. "Man, you see how easy the steak knife goes through it?" The guy teased Bryson as he prepped his steak for demolition. "I see you man! I'm 'bout to get the same one." Just as Bryson finished makin' the statement, the waitress came to take our order.

After we ordered, Bryson started talkin' about the incident from the ball. I was glad he brought it up first 'cuz the whole time I sat there in silence not knowin' what to say. I wasn't sure how to start a conversation because of all the drama we'd just left. I mean, if he were a "for sure" for the rest of the night, then I would have made an effort to start idol conversation until we got to the room to complete the "business transaction." But, my mind was made about how the night would end back at the room when Bryson changed clothes. So, that bein' said; there really wasn't much more for us to talk about besides "current" events. "Man! This shit is crazy Berry." Bryson held his head down like he was overwhelmed. "Nigga's just think they can disrespect me *and* my date like I'm not shit! I'm so sick of these ol' ass wanna be pimp nigga's." Bryson took a sip of his water. I just continued to listen to him vent. "I'm tellin' you Berry, if that nigga "Cal" come with some bullshit...." He stopped and shook his head in disbelief. "Who is "Cal" Bryson? I'd remembered Bot makin' reference to "Cal" findin' out, but I didn't know who they were talkin' about. Bryson's pager went off. "See, here we go with this bullshit!" He placed the pager on vibrate and sat it on the table. "How long have you been in this game Berry?" Bryson questioned me as if my inquiry to him was a thing of the past. I was reluctant to answer his question. But, he was referred through Cassie, so it wasn't like he couldn't get the information anyway. "About a little over a year now." I lied. Actually, I pretty much started right after I graduated from high school. It was closer to two years, but the last year had been more concurrent. I figured I'd give him just enough to pacify his curiosity and prevent him from havin' a reason to pump Cassie for information. "Well, you need to stop!" Now I was offended and irritated by Bryson trying to tell me what I should and shouldn't be doin'. He's got a lot of nerves. If it weren't for the freaky ass men out there seekin' women like me, escorts; not hoes, then we'd all be out of business. He asked for me; which means he is *willin' to pay for the ass* just like the rest of them that feel the need to have a variety. Some were married with kids on the way, some had girlfriends, and some had lovers. Although I didn't know exactly where Bryson fell on that scale, he was *still* willin' to pay for an extremely good fuck. Now he wants to tell me I need to stop? "Yeah right", I thought to myself. I guess he could see the irritation on my face because he tried to clean his comment up by sayin', "This game don't need newcomers like you Berry. You're a lovely young lady with family that cares about you. You're smart and got a good head on your shoulders. This game ain't for you. It's too many snakes in the green grass sitting back waiting to just jump out and bite you on your sexy little plump ass!" My irritation erupted, "How you gone tell me about this "game" not bein' for me? From the looks of it, you're the one that's not cut out for this! I grabbed my water and took a sip with my face frowned up. "I didn't mean to offend you Berry, I'm just saying..." I interjected, "you're just sayin' WHAT Bryson? Look, I don't need your advice because things ain't goin' "peachy" for you right now. Ok, I realize that you took up for me and everything, but I can handle my own. In case you haven't noticed, I'M GROWN! Bot don't scare me! I was ready for his ass. If you hadn't took up for me it still would have been done. Madame already told me if I had a problem with anybody, male or female, to let her know and she would take care of it." Bryson choked on his water. *Madame?!"* He said her name with a look of disgust on his face. "Madame told you if you have a problem to let her know and she would take care of it?" He laughed as he talked to me. "Madame *is* the fucking enemy Berry!" A look of shock was on Bryson's face as he looked at me as if I were clueless. He was right! I was completely clueless to his observation of Madame and his analysis of her comment. "How can you say that? Madame was the one that told me you were a "good guy" when she stopped me in the restroom. She had nothin' but good things to say about you. I figured that was the reason that she said if anybody messes with me to let her know. I *thought* she was lookin' out for me on the strength of y'all relationship." Bryson just sat there starin' at me with this look of pity and disbelief on his face. I was uncomfortable with his pathetic glare. "Why are you lookin' at me like that Bryson?" He hesitated. "Yeah, you're *half* right! That crazy bitch was lookin' out for you; to a certain extent Berry, but it *definitely* wasn't on the strength of me. That's for sure."

Ok, so now things are goin' through my head as I am attackin' the steak bites grilled in sautéed onions and mushrooms, seasoned to perfection and layin' right next to the potato skins covered in a mixture of American and mozzarella cheese, with bacon bits and chives sprinkled all over them. "Damn! This food is good as hell!' Bryson chuckled, "Ain't it though?" His pager was vibratin' on the table in front of him. After about the first eight times it went off, he stopped lookin' at the number displayed.

Considerin' he'd requested my services from Cassie, I figured he had to be getting money some other way in order to be associated with pimps and ballers. Right? It hit me that even though I never got personal with a client, I always found out which category they fell in. Come to think of it, Cassie just showed me a picture of him. She never did divulge much information on him. My mind is clickin' now and it showed on my face. "Damn! You lookin' all serious eating that cheese stick. What you tryin' to do, figure out the ingredients!" Bryson was crackin' up. He must of thought that corny shit was funny. I could have easily cracked back in him by on him by askin' him if his balls were thirsty since he didn't put any water on 'em but right now, I got too many questions to ask and ain't got time to be laughin'. "So, how did you find out about me?" I wiped my mouth as I waited for Bryson's reply. Bryson sat his glass of water on the table after he took a 'squig' and wiped his mouth. He leaned across the table so he wouldn't have to shout over Chaka Kahn's *Through The Fire* playin' in the background. "I called Cassie and she referred you." Ok, so of course the next question to roll off my tongue would be…."How long have you known Cassie?" Bryson was Johhny-on-the-spot with his answer. "One of my colleagues referred me to her." That response was so broad it left me no room to narrow anything down. I can't ask him about who his colleague is and how this person knows Cassie without makin' myself seem suspicious. Bryson picked up his pager after it started buzzing by the plate. He shook his head and had an uneasy look on his face. I was waitin' for him to ask me why I was askin him how he knew Cassie, but he never said anything else behind his reply. I guess the person pagin' him threw him off. Just as Bryson sat his pager down, my pager buzzed in my purse as I opened it to stash a few of the wet wipes they'd given us with our meals. When I pulled it out, the display showed that Cassie had paged me twice. "That's strange." I thought to myself after I put the pager back in my purse. Cassie had never paged me when I was out workin'. I would be the one callin' her if something wasn't right like I'd done in the past. "Is everything ok here?" The waitress refilled our waters as she hustled for her tip. "Everything is straight. Bryson answered for both of us. Ummm, where is the ladies room?" I stood up as the waitress pointed to the back of the room. Bryson stood up from the table to excuse me. Just as I thought! There was a payphone in the back of the restaurant between the ladies and the men's room. I picked up the receiver and put my quarter in. "Hello?" I spoke first because the ringin' stopped but nobody said anything. "Berry?" Cassie acted like she couldn't catch the voice on the other end of her receiver. How many people had she paged twice besides me? "Yeah, I just saw you paged me twice. What's up?" I braced myself for her response. I don't know why, but I just figured it was bad news. Cassie never called me while I was out. "Oh! Ummm, I was just calling to see if you talked to Jeremy?" Now my heart is beati' fast as hell. Cassie and Jeremy have a good relationship as far as I've seen. I mean, they get into it every now and then, but it was usually Cassie that was mad at Jeremy all the time. She would have talked to him more recently than me. Jeremy and I live together. We see and talk to each other when we get home. We've never made random calls throughout the day just to see what each other were doin'. "What's the problem Cassie?" I was irritated by now playing this game with Cassie. "D*aang*! Calm down Berry! Everything is ok. I got mad at him and he wouldn't return my call. This is him on the other line now." I slammed the payphone receiver down on the phone and went in the restroom to freshen up. My makeup needed to be reapplied and the frown on my face needed to be adjusted. When I got back to the table, Bryson wasn't there. I'd eaten so much that I couldn't force myself to eat another bite. I would definitely be comin' back to this place. *Caper's* had some bomb ass food!

Just as I picked my water up to flush down the food I demolished, there was a tap on my shoulder. "Berry?" I turned around and was shocked to see the familiar face callin' out my name. "Myron?" I could not believe my eyes! It was Myron; Mitchell's identical twin brother. We hadn't seen each other since we were kids playing in church. I would ask sistah Beulah about him whenever I saw her, which had been awhile because I'd been away from church for so long. Usually when she would come see momma, I'd be walkin' out the door either leavin' to go shoppin' with Cassie, or on my way to "work." The last time I asked about him, sister Beulah seemed a bit stand-offish to my inquiries. Myron grabbed me and gave me the biggest hug. It felt so good to finally be in his arms like I'd fantasized about all those years ago. He had on a pair of light blue Karl Kani jeans and a nice Versace shirt that had blue, green and black swirls in it. His cologne had the smell of musk and stood out just like his dark features and good looks. It dawned on me how much he and Mitchell really looked alike. I could always tell them apart, but it hit me that they really did have the *same* face although their personalities stood apart from one another. "So, how have you been?" He smiled and his dimples pierced through his cheeks. I wanted to hurry up and end the conversation before Bryson came back into the restaurant. I did *not* want Myron to see me with another guy, let alone Bryson. Although Myron had been outta town since before the night of Angelo's murder at my party, there was no tellin' if he already knew Bryson or knew *about* him. Mitchell was up there in the game and he and Jeremy did business all the time. Which means Mitchell knows Cassie and since Mitchell is Myron's brother and I'm Jeremy's sister; there was just too many parties involved for my secret to remain uncovered. "I've been great! Just tryin' to keep myself busy until school starts." My heart raced as the lie rolled off my tongue. I had to think fast before he asked "What school?" If I stumbled over my words Myron would know I was lyin'. I'd been out of high school for a while now; never even thought to sign up for college. There was too much I was dealin' with already, and besides.... I didn't need an education to help me with finances for the future. My finances were just fine and my appearance reflected it. As far as I was concerned, I was "tight". "Oh, you're about to go to school? That's good Berry!" He touched my shoulder as he congratulated me. I had goose bumps all over my body. My nipples were standin' at attention like two soldiers in front of a commandin' officer! I folded my arms in an attempt to camouflage my missiles. "So, I won't interrupt you. I know you're not here alone. Here, take down my number and give me a call. I'll be here for a couple of weeks on assignment." Myron passed me a pen and grabbed a napkin off the empty table behind him. My mind had its way with him as he leaned over me while I wrote down the 10 digits he called out. Ooooo, he smelled so damn good! His curly black hair trimmed on the top, tapered around the sides. "You still look nice!" Myron whispered seductively in my ear as I wrote the last number. "Thank you; so do you!" I replied softly." My heart was racin'. Feelin's of warmth, anxiety and butterflies took over. After all these years I am *still* attracted to him the way I was back in the day. He could definitely have me at NO cost! Before he walked away I was sure to check his left hand for evidence of commitment. No ring, no tan line! "Make *sure* you call me Berry." I put the number in my purse and replied, "I will Myron." Yes Myron, "I will." The words I said a million times in the mirror as a child dreaming he and I were gettin' married. He disappeared to the back of the room to the table closest to the bar joining a female and another man. Just as Myron left, Bryson hurried through the front door, up the stairs to our table in the "red carpet" section. "C'mon Berry! I need to take you back to the hotel." He tossed a hundred dollar bill outta the wad in his hand. The waitress hadn't even come to cash us out yet. Bryson grabbed my arm and hurried me along as I scrambled for my purse on the table.

Once we were in the parkin' lot I asked, "What's the rush Bryson? What's wrong?" Bryson closed my door and scurried along to the driver's side. "Nothing.", he replied. "I just need to take care of something." Bryson's jumpy actions made me leery of him. Something *had* to be wrong because he burned rubber as we exited the parkin' lot turnin' onto Gratiot.

Root of All Evil

SOME THINGS WE DO WE CANNOT CHANGE
SO I HAD TO ASK MYSELF, "IS THIS WORTH
THE STREET FAME?"
THE WAY THAT I ABANDONED MY FAITH;
DEGRADED MY NAME
I HOLD MY HEAD DOWN IN SHAME

The more I made the more I craved to stand on top
No realizing that eventually I would *have* to stop
Because doing it this way, I was sure to get popped or
dropped
But either way I'm bound to do a belly-up flop

I think about that "one" day that I may suffer the
cruelest of pain
Now I start to falter at what I'm doing
It's become such an unbearable strain

I pray for His help NOW because it is now that I lack
But I can't seem to count all my blessings
So I guess He turned His back
At least I can say I've lived the "life" with all the cash, cars & honey's,
But it was destroyed in the end by the Root of All Evil;
The love I that I had for my money

D'Aviér

Moment In history

My life took many turns those past 5 years. The choices I made ended up bein' much like a stack of dominoes fallin' fast after a cat's tail mistakenly bumped up against them. After the first wrong irrational decision that went against everything my mother had taught us, Jeremy & I just started to make more and more bad decisions in an effort to somehow clean up those made prior. The house was saved by our grandparents. After my granddad passed, my grandmother ended up going into a nursin' home. She'd been diagnosed with Dementia, a common disease amongst the elderly that somehow attacks their memory.

With all the money Jeremy once stacked and the money I accumulated, we should have been able to maintain that house and a neighbor's house! But, my bother ended up becomin' a victim of his own product. Eventually, word got out that he was gettin' high & had been for quite some time before Cassie & I even found out. His frequent trips to the garage, nose bleeds, erratic "lows" and constant paranoia made me & momma suspicious until he *mistakenly* burned the garage down. After that he had no choice but to admit he was an addict. Some nights he would literally lock himself in the garage, and snort as many rows as he could. The drug paraphernalia among the debris during the fire inspection spoke volumes; not to mention the dumb ass look on his face when momma to kicked the door and found Jeremy face down on the table with a plate full of pure cocaine under his damn nose. It seems like as soon as we pulled him out, the small fire around him ignited into flames that hit the ceilin' with force & fury. There goes our low key family reputation; 'cuz just like the flames spread....... so did the gossip about Jeremy bein' the cause of it. Of course by the time sistah Beulah got wind of the story, she decided to stop by and share what she heard, and of course pick up a some "to go" gossip for the road. Yeah, this gossip and drama would definitely serve to be greater than the Tirianna's brutal death; the death that everybody in the hood, except sistah Beulah, saw comin' many years before it happened. Tirianna was a full-fledged *whore*. Turnin' tricks in cars with her so called "boyfriends" eventually turned into, standin' on the corner as a prostitute. She wasn't makin' much money, so her pimp would constantly beat her up. She had more black eyes than a bag of peas! She'd been around the hood so much that there wasn't one male left that hadn't fucked her already; maybe even three or four times. Her body was found in an abandon building over on Pitkin Street in Highland Park. She was naked, beaten, and her hands were cut off at the wrists. The medical examiner's couldn't tell if she'd been raped or not; either because there was no semen, or too much due to of her line of work. Damon was the first to unremorsefully break the news to me and momma. Their family had pretty much disowned her after most of their valuables had disappeared from the house. Tawana, the nicer of the twins and Lynette were both married and had families and careers. Lynette is a scientologist and Tawana is a pediatric nurse over at Sinai Grace Hospital on Outer Drive. The last of the Mohicans in Sister Beulah's family, Myron and Mitchell, weren't doin' so bad either. Mitchell went from street pharmacist to business man. He took his drug money and invested in his dad's car company. Perelli's Auto sold cars in the neighborhood to the less fortunate who would have otherwise not been able to afford a brand new or mildly worn car due to no credit or bad credit. They even accepted food stamps for down payments! Mitchell's arrogant attitude diminished over time and he and I were quite pleasant to one another before he relocated to Denver, CO to open the next car lot. I eventually found out from Devine that Myron was an FBI agent! He'd left fresh out of high school to attend Michigan State University. Once he finished his Masters in criminology, he applied for the FBI. He passed with flyin' colors and received a promotion as head of Narcotics and Distribution. I never would have thought that I would end up bein' in protective custody because of my family "ties" and the people I'd surrounded myself with. If it weren't for DeAngelo's grandmother, Devine, keepin' me up *on* game *in* the game, I would have never found out that Bryson, officially my LAST client in the escorting business, was workin' for Calvin! Yeah, Calvin; the one that was road dogs with my dad. The same Calvin that always seemed to care about my mother, Jeremy and I. The man that befriended my brother and got him hooked on drugs after he stole my brother's major connects by feedin' them lies and spittin' venom on our family name. That same Calvin paid Bryson to sleep with me and get nude pictures of girl's that wouldn't give in to his flashy attire, fancy cars and promises of how he would take care of them for life if they "worked" for him. It was ironically *thee same* Calvin that we ended up hearin' rumors about how he not only set DeAngelo up to be killed at my party, but also killed Tirianna because she wasn't makin' him any more money on the streets. She pocketed a *measly* twenty dollars so she could feed her habit and he'd did *all that killin'* to that girl; just *overkilled* her. That same Calvin threatened to kill Bryson's pregnant girlfriend if he didn't sleep with me and get a naked picture of me so he could use it as proof to show moma and Jeremy if I wasn't on payroll at the escort service he wanted me to run. Calvin came on to me one day when he stopped by to "check" on Jeremy. "So, you ready to stop playin' hoe and start make 'n me some doe?" I acted like I didn't know what he was talkin' about. "You playin' with wolves little sheep!" He grabbed me by the neck of my blouse and pulled me closer to him. I yanked back and grabbed the closest thing I could find. "Get the fuck off of me Calvin", I yelled. Momma and Jeremy had been out with Damon lookin' at the house Damon was trying to buy with his drug profits. I stood there with the box cutter that Jeremy had left on the counter. "Ha, ha, ha, ha,ha! You really think you're tough don't you Berry? He reached behind him and pulled out a .32 revolver and held it up in my face. "Yeah, I hear you're a real **pussy** cat in bed!" He rubbed the barrel of the gun alongside my face and down my cleavage as he grabbed my hair with the other hand. "Meow bitch! 'Cuz the dog in me is about to tear your ass up!" Calvin slapped the box cutter out of my hand, turned me around and forced my pants and panties down. Tears rolled down my eyes and my heart was beatin' fast again. "Lord! Please don't let this..." Just as I began my prayer, I could hear Jeremy's key turning in the door. Jeremy, momma and Damon were walking in and momma called my name. "Berry? Come and get this bag!" Calvin quickly placed his semi-erect penis back in his boxers. He placed his revolver in his back. I pulled my pants and panties up in a nick of time as

Damon appeared in the kitchen doorway. "My bad! Damn! I didn't know y'all was in here. What's up Berry?" I'd barely finished wiping the tears from my face. "Nothin' much Damon." My voice shook with anger &fear. "Everything alright in here?" Damon glanced and me and then stared at Calvin. He'd already had his suspicions about Calvin's relationship with Jeremy from the beginning. Damon would always say, "It's just something about that nigga that I don't like." But Jeremy would always try to convince Damon that Calvin was cool peeps 'cuz of his relationship with our parent over the years. "I'm cool Damon. 'Bout to go take a shower real quick and freshen up. I just feel so sticky and dirty." I said it sarcastically. "Yeah, I can see how you would feel that way. It seems a little "hot" in here to me too for some reason." Damon returned the sarcasm I'd directed in reference to Calvin. "Actually, I'm about to go 'n here and holler at Jeremy and Brandy before I leave." Calvin must have felt the ray of death Damon was visually shootin' at him. "Berry, don't forget about that. I'll keep you posted on the details." Calvin walked out of the kitchen just as cool and smooth as he'd walked in. Damon walked over to me. "You alright Berry? You do know that I care about you and there is nothing that you can't tell me, right?" He brushed the hair back from my face. "I know Damon." Tears began to form in my eyes but I held them back. I brushed past him and headed out of the kitchen. As I was leavin' Jeremy was comin' in. "What's up Berry?" Jeremy didn't think anything was wrong, he just greeted me that way whenever he hadn't seen me for a few hours. "Nothin' Jeremy; bout to go take a shower." I walked past him with my head down. Once I got to the steps I could hear momma and Calvin talkin'. "I don't think it's anything to be worried about Calvin. Berry is grown now and she and Damon grew up together. If there was something goin' on and especially if he were mistreatin' Berry, Jeremy and I would have known by now. Are my ears deceivin' me? This snake ass nigga just tried to fuckin' *rape* me in MY house and now he has the nerves to be tryin' to convince my momma that Damon is the bad guy? You have got to be fuckin kiddin' me!

It wasn't long after that kitchen incident that I was informed about all the other ties Calvin had. Divine had been schoolin' me on some things after Bryson disappeared. Bryson hadn't been seen since the night he dropped me off back at the hotel we'd met at. Out of concern, I'd tried to contact him on the number I had, but there was never an answer or a return phone call. About a week after his disappearance, Myron paid a visit to our house in an unmarked car with a younger guy who had a very familiar face. Just so happens I was comin' out the house when they walked up. Before he told me the real nature of his visit, he kinda appeared to have been concerned with the family and everybody's well-being. After that, it was ALL business. Myron introduced his partner and I couldn't help but stare. That's when it hit me! Myron's partner was the SAME guy at the hotel! The guy who valet parked my car. He and Myron had been watchin' my comin's and goin's for quite some time. At first I thought it was relatin' to Jeremy, but as the conversation went on they started showin' me mug shots and givin' me bits of information in the form of evidence Myron and his partner actually KNEW about Jeremy and his line of business, but they were MORESO concerned with the individuals that we allowed into our surroundings. Their main concern was Calvin and his female accomplice, also known as....... Cassie! It seems Ms. Shady Ass Cassie was the one bitch Calvin used to get close to Jeremy once he found out how prosperous Jeremy was at the hustling weight. Since Calvin had the money and bitches, he wanted to expand into drugs. People knew how shady he was but wouldn't dare speak of it because of his ruthless background. So, Calvin MADE nigga's deal with him on that level and if they weren't tearin' him off a percentage of the profit, he would fuck them over....just like he did DeAngelo. That was the reason Divine moved so quickly after DeAngelo's death. She'd heard on the streets that Calvin was actually the one that put the hit out on Angelo. And to show you how much this bastard cared about my dead father, (may he rest in peace), my strugglin' mother and her two kids that he'd seen grow into a adults, he *purposely* had that shit done at my sweet sixteen birthday party! BASTARD!

Cassie wasn't so innocent either. I was wonderin' why this bitch just KEPT askin' me had I heard anything from Bryson after out last date. The more I told her connivin' ass "NO," she would still ask after a couple days. Well, according to Myron and his partner, they'd seen Calvin leavin' Cassie's apartment at all times of the day and night. He stayed for long periods and sometimes even overnight. It was Calvin's mastermind that made Cassie turn me on to the escort business. My dumb ass fell for the bait! Cassie's mom was never in an insane asylum either. The "head" bitch at the Baller's party Bryson and I attended was Cassie's mom! Yes, "Madame" is Cassie's mother! She's the same lady that knew who I was before we'd even been introduced; the lady that told me if I needed *anything* to let her know. This was the lady that Divine seemed to bow down to in the ladies room….. it all started to make sense to me now. Cassie's mom and Calvin were lovers back in the day, right after Cassie's dad left. So technically, Calvin was like Cassie's stepdad; or at least she looked up to him as a stepdad until he started molestin' and eventually rapin' her repeatedly while her mom was out trickin' for him. Cassie tried to tell her mother but by then her mom was in too deep with Calvin and never had time for Cassie. Calvin's old slick ass ended up flippin' everything by convincin' Madame that Cassie tried to come on to him. I kind of started feeling sorry and empathetic for Cassie 'cuz I never knew that Calvin was screwin' both of them under the same roof. My head was SCRAMBLED after hearin' this shit! I thought I would faint; but THEN, I heard the ultimate shocker! The night DeAngelo was killed; Cassie and Calvin were laid up….. TOGETHER. Cassie was *fully* aware of the hit and told not to come to the party. She was instructed to take me shoppin', drop my ass off, and keep it movin'; which she did. I was FURIOUS with all of the information I was gettin', yet thankful that I was informed when I was. It was also said that before Bryson went M.I.A (missin' in action), he'd been anonymously callin' the feds, dry snitchin', to let them know that Calvin was puttin' hits on people left and right. Who calls the FEDS *"anonymous?"* That explains why I ended up bumpin' into Myron that night at *Capers*. They were followin' us due to a tip they'd gotten from Bryson about the blackmail that Calvin was holdin' over his head. This mess was truly an eye opener for me and it gave me the opportunity to finally make a RATIONAL decision in my life. Bryson left the restaurant in a hurry because Calvin called him and told him he was "Next" and then hung up the phone. BOT was workin' with Calvin, but didn't know how deep Calvin was into this game.

So, after the shit hit the fan, I was offered to go into protective custody because the FBI had more than enough to go on in order to build a criminal case against Calvin for murder, solicitation, tax evasion and a number of other things. Calvin's days were numbered..... in more ways than one. I'd promised to go into protective custody but only after a few of my demands be granted. I needed them to not press criminal charges on Jeremy and to allow him to get the help he needed to get off drugs. I also requested that momma *not* be informed of any information regardin' this pendin' case against Calvin & Cassie. I just didn't need momma worryin' more than she already had over the years. Tears started to form in my eyes. Man, if I go into protective custody, I knew I wouldn't be able to talk to or see to Jeremy and momma until Calvin and Cassie were convicted and sentenced. It was a hard decision for me, but I knew I had to do what was best for me and my family. First, I had a few things to take care of and I KNEW just the people that would help. "How long will I have before it's time for me to turn myself in?" I asked Myron out of curiosity so I could focus on how much time I had to make my next move. "Well, considerin' that you know all the details now, we'd like to take you NOW! This way we won't be investigating your death or Jeremy's & Mrs. Brandy's." My eyebrows turned up. "Don't worry Berry. I'll make sure nothing happens to you and the family. I have your back just like I did when we were younger. And besides, my brother comes through here frequently. I know what

Jeremy and Damon *both* do out here, but I turn a deaf ear and a blind eye to it because this is what a lot of people who grew up in the hood *have* to do to survive. Everybody couldn't be as fortunate as me and go to college." Myron smiled at me and brought back so many memories of our childhood and my crush on him. "I know you do Myron. So, are you gonna get my brother some help? I have money saved to put towards his recovery, but its money from the 'business', and I don't want any problems." Myron bit his bottom lip exposin' his dimples. "Ok, we'll make sure Jeremy gets the help he needs Berry. Save your money and invest in what you wanna do after all of this is taken care of. Jeremy and you will be able to live a normal life with a clean slate once it's all said and done Berry."

I only had 2 days to call Myron & give the "ok" to go into protective custody, but only because I knew Myron personally. I talked him into givin' me a week. I told him that I wanted to make sure Jeremy was checked into rehab before I went into hidin' and that momma was safe because Myron and I both knew that getting' her to leave Mckinley would be like pullin' teeth from a hungry bull! We knew she would never go for it and that all of this was sure to make her have a stroke worrying about Jeremy and I. We both agree that Calvin wouldn't no match for momma when it came to her kids. But, because her health was of concern, we felt it wouldn't be wise to jeopardize it by fillin' her in on this whole investigation. She'd just come to grips with Jeremy's addiction and the garage bein' burned down as a result of it. So, that's where Damon came in. Once Myron allowed me to fill Damon in on the investigation of Cassie and Calvin, Damon agreed to stay at the house with momma as an added security measure. He was prepared to kill on sight if Calvin even *thought* to come over. But, of course we played it cool around Myron insistin' Damon would call him IMMEDIATELY if Calvin or Cassie came over. I lied and told momma that I would check Jeremy into rehab somewhere in Madison Heights, MI and get a room there for his first 30 days so she wouldn't have to worry about his progress and tryin' to drive out there regularly to see him. I assured her that I would call her frequently with updates and that once Jeremy finished the first 30 days, he would be able to contact her himself. Truth was, Jeremy would be in Madison Heights, but I wouldn't be with him. Jeremy was ready to get help. I guess the whole embarrassment of the garage and being discovered the way he was by momma and I was enough to finally make him want to get himself together. Damon, Myron, and I all felt it was best to not inform Jeremy of the situation at hand and the fact that he would be under protective custody in rehab as well. He wasn't in the right frame of mind to deal with all that was goin' on. Plus, with the way he'd become close to Calvin, we didn't want to risk the chance of Jeremy revealin' anything to Calvin until all charges were brought up against him and the evidence and witnesses were secured. I had one week to put a plan in action. Over the next two days I would be busy as hell. I made a few phone calls, figured out my key players, and put my plan in action. By day three, Jeremy and I were cryin' and sayin' our good-byes to one another. We both hugged and kissed momma, told her we loved her and promised that we would be home as soon as Jeremy was allowed home visits for the weekend after completin' the first two of the ten step program he was enterin'. We both knew we wouldn't be able to see momma for at least 3 weeks of the 10 weeks we were supposed to be in protective custody. Only me and Damon knew that Jeremy and I wouldn't be allowed to call momma for the whole ten weeks. I had never been away from my mother for any long periods of time and I really couldn't get a grip on doin' it now; especially since I wouldn't be able to talk to her. Man, after Jeremy and I rode off, I cried like a baby...... and so did Jeremy!

Once Jeremy had been officially checked in, we hugged like neither of us wanted to let go. "You know I love you Berry?" Jeremy was more emotional today than I'd ever seen him in my entire life. "I know Jeremy." I was tryin' not to just burst out and tell Jeremy everything that was goin' on as I fought back the tears that somehow seemed to escape from my face anyway. "Don't worry big brother, we'll make it through this. The McDaniel family has gotten through some of the worst, so this is small potatoes!" I managed to talk in my "God Father" voice just to make light of the situation. It worked! Jeremy burst into laughter. "That's my little Merry Berry! Who would have ever thought you'd be comin' to my rescue one day? Are you your Brother's Keeper?" Jeremy reflected on a scene from the movie *New Jack City*. "Yes! I *AM* my Brother's Keeper", I replied. Jeremy chuckled as he looked me in my eyes and said, "You just remember who pulled you in that little red wagon to get them free government lunches back in the day. I'm gone kick this shit Berry and we gone have a **bunch** of laughs about this shit one day. Hey, I did manage to hold on to about three g's.

Check in momma's room in the taped up shoe box under her dresser. I hid it from myself so I wouldn't go down with nothin'. I told Damon to make sure you got it if something were to happen to me. I was talkin' about a nigga poppin' me or if I went to jail, but I guess this would be another occasion where you would "break the glass" in case of an emergency." The people at the front desk were callin' for Jeremy to go behind the double grey doors to get started on his detox. "Oh, call Calvin and let him know where I am. That nigga owe me some cash I loaned him about six months ago. He was supposed to be payin' me back in a couple weeks but I forgot all about it. Oh, and don't tell momma yet 'cuz I want it to be a surprise when I get out of here, but Cassie is twelve weeks pregnant with my baby; she called and told me she went to the doctor yesterday. Call her and tell her I love her and I'mma be 'right' so I can see my lil man or princess grow up! Matter of fact, just tell Calvin to give her the money he owes me so she won't have to worry about me doin' somethin' crazy with it. That money will take care of the baby for a nice minute." I stood there blank faced for a minute with my mouth opened. "Berry? You hear me?" WOW! My brother had no clue that this bitch Cassie could possibly be pregnant by Calvin and that she and Calvin were about to go to jail for a long ass time once the "feds" got a hold to their asses. DAMN! I wanna tell him so bad, but I can't. "Jeremy?" I said as calm as possible. "Just out of curiosity, how much money will Calvin be expected to give Cassie as repayment to you?" I spoke with clarity so my brother wouldn't have to read between the lines like he often tried to do. "thirty-five hundred to be exact, but I gave him product and cash combined. He said he needed to pay somebody and he would double it and give five hundred extra in interest; altogether that's seventy-five hundred. So, make sure you call him 'cuz Cassie's gonna need it for your little niece or nephew." "Mr. McDaniels? We're ready for you, NOW!" The lady in scrubs called for Jeremy one last time. She seemed irritated that he didn't respond the first time. "OK, Jeremy. I tell Cassie and Calvin both if I see them….. I mean *when* I see them." Jeremy blew me a kiss and headed toward the double grey doors where the nurse's assistant stood waitin' impatiently. My brother walked away with the understandin' that I would be about two miles down at the Best Western Hotel in Madison Heights. He also trusted that I would take care of his business with Calvin and Cassie for him. He was about half right.

I scrambled for time as I left the detox/rehabilitation place. I made a quick phone call to Damon tellin' him to open the back door when he got the next call from me tomorrow night. After we hung up, I placed a quick call to Devine and my plan was now officially a plot. If the cards were played right, this would be a cinch just like Damon and Devine assured me it would be. As I pulled up in the gated community where Devine lived….. The gate was opened and the car she'd had an out of town relative to rent was sittin' in the circular driveway…. Doors opened, keys in the ignition, gloves in the glove box…..just as we'd planned.

Day four, I was at the house packin' my clothes preparin' to go into protective custody for ten weeks. Momma was sittin' in the kitchen drinkin' coffee and doing a word puzzle. I'd informed momma that Jeremy was in good spirits when I left him about an hour ago and that I would call her once I got back to the hotel. I told her that I came home to get a few items I'd forgotten when Jeremy and I left. As I walked out of the kitchen, Damon was comin' down from *my* bedroom. I looked confused as we gave each other eye contact. "What?" Damon had this dumb look on his face like he knew what I was about to say. "I know you didn't think I was gone sleep in Jeremy's dirty ass room!" I snickered and said, "Well, yeah…. I can definitely understand that! Hey, keep momma busy for a minute. I gotta get that box Jeremy told me about in her room." Damon smiled sneakily. "It's in your room under the bed! I figured he would be tellin' you to get it so I moved it last night." If I never knew anything about Jeremy's friends, I knew for sure that DeAngelo and Damon were two down ass nigga's that had mad love for my brother and my family. I smiled. "Good lookin' out!" Damon returned the smile as he spoke to me with his eyes and replied, "Anything for you Berry! Seriously, there's nothing you can't ask me for and not get it."

The next forty minutes or so were spent killin time and puttin' Damon up on Calvin borrowin' money from Jeremy along with the whole Cassie is pregnant bullshit. I'd already contacted Myron and told him to have the unmarked car and his partner to come and pick me up from momma's house. I would tell momma that a friend was pickin' me up for dinner before I went back to the hotel. She would have no choice but to believe me. She hadn't *caught* me in a lie as of yet. If she had, I would have been the FIRST to know about it! I left Damon in the living room and followed momma into the bedroom. Momma and I talked about how we both hoped Jeremy would get himself together and reminisced on the past as Jeremy and I grew over the years and all the cute and dumb stuff we'd done as children.   About ten minutes into our conversation, there was a knock at the door. Momma didn't even move from her spot. She'd grown accustomed to Damon bein' there with her. She knew Damon would get to the door before her. "That young man watches over me like he's *my* son instead of Beulah's! I can't get up to get a glass of water without him bringin' it to me time he THINK I'm thirsty!" Momma and I both laughed as I got up off her bed and readjusted my clothes.   "Well ma, that's probably my ride. I'mma call you when I get to the hotel after I go check on Jeremy." I hugged momma and kissed the top of her head as she sat up in bed. "Love you ma." She kissed me back and told me she loved me too. Just as I was about to exit the bedroom, there stood Damon.   "Damn! You scared me Damon!" I held my chest and bent over like it was hurtin'. "My bad Berry, but Myron stopped by and said he wanted to see you before you leave out. I turned and looked at momma to see what her reaction would be. "Tell Myron I said hello! I ain't seen him since he left for college. I saw him out there talkin' to Berry the other day; thought he was comin' in, but I guess he had something to do 'cuz he left when he finished talkin' to her." Damon and I did a quick glance at each other. I was at a loss of words, but Damon interjected, "Ok Mrs. Brandy. I'll tell him, but I know he said he wanted to holler at Berry before he goes to work. He'll be back though 'cuz we're supposed to be pickin' up Tirianna's head stone from the Funeral Parlor." Whew! Sweat was beadin' on my forehead! "Ok baby! Be sure to tell Beulah I'm here if she needs me. I couldn't imagine how I would feel if I lost one of my kids. I know it's really got to be takin' its toll on her." Momma sat there shakin' her head at the thought of what sistah Beulah must have been going through by losin' her daughter.... A twin at that! I eased out of momma's bedroom with Damon followin' close behind me. "I thought he was sendin' his partner in an unmarked car?" I spoke through my teeth and under my breath. "Calm down Berry....relax! Everything is alright." Damon spoke low and calm. "Hey Myron, I'm ready." I grabbed my overnight bag with the money in it and a few other miscellaneous items. "Ummm Berry?" Myron held his head down and hesitated. "Well, sometime last night we got a call about an alarm goin' off at a residence in Pontiac. When officers responded to the call by the ADT dispatcher, they arrived at a house engulfed in flames. Once the fire was tamed and eventually put out, fire fighter's going through the debris discovered the corpses of a black male in his early fifties and a female in her late 20's. Those bodies have been identified as Cassie & Calvin!" My mouth hit the floor! "WH...WHAT?" I asked as if it were too much for me to comprehend. Myron proceeded, "Yeah, it looks like somebody got to them before we did. Not sure what the motive was, but what we do know is that they both have a list of people that COULD be persons of interest or suspects!" I held my head and closed my eyes as if I couldn't take anymore. "Oh My God! I can NOT believe this shit!" I didn't want to overdo it, but I had to make it seem real. "Myron, Jeremy just told me two days that Cassie was bein' blackmailed!" Myron's eyebrow rose as he pulled out his writin' tablet. "Did he really?" He began to take notes. "So, did he say anything to you about who she thought was blackmailing her or why she was bein' blackmailed? I pondered over his question purposely. "Ummmm, no; not that I know of. Jeremy really wasn't around her like that. I mean, she would come to the house and chill; sometimes even overnight, but for the most part, Jeremy stayed in the garage or on the streets husslin'. Myron continued to write and never looked up from his notebook. He continued with his line of questionin'. "So, until we came around you with the information, you had no idea that Cassie and Calvin were an item?" I didn't know where Myron was goin' with these questions, but I hung on to each word; replayin' them in my head in an effort to answer them correctly without puttin' my foot in my mouth. "Of course not Myron!" My voice was low and squeaky as if I were about to cry. "That's my brother! Come on nah'! If I KNEW Cassie was cheatin' on him or suspected she was with ANYBODY; I don't care if it was Santa Claus, I would have been the FIRST to let my brother know!" I must have sounded convincin' enough 'cuz Myron shook his head in agreement. "O.K. Berry, I understand." Myron looked at me with those brown eyes and pierced my soul. If he'd had x-ray vision, he would have been able to see my heart skippin' beats after every question he asked. "Weren't you and Cassie business partners?" I knew I couldn't lie 'cuz I'd seen Myron on duty at Caper's the last night I saw Bryson. I know he'd had all kinds of information on me, so this was definitely something I wouldn't be able to get out of. "Yes! Cassie would set me with different clients to decorate for different events or to pick up the deposits they'd out down to book me. I whispered just in case Damon was somewhere within ear shot of Myron's and my conversation. I lied in an effort to keep my 'clean girl' reputation so Myron wouldn't get the wrong impression of me. The last thing I need was for him to equate me as the same type of whore his sister Tirianna was. Either I picked up the remainin' balance or Cassie would but I gave her her portion of the money for gettin' me clients at various places. Myron continued to write and ask questions. "So, you trusted her word that the money she was givin' you was ALL the money she'd gotten from these….uhhhh "clients?" It seemed as if Myron was hintin' around to somethin' or like he didn't believe me. But, I stuck to my story and answered each question without much hesitation…..just as I practiced with Devine. "Listen Myron, I don't know where you're goin' with these questions, but I NEVER had a reason to NOT trust Cassie. She's looked out for me on NUMEROUS occasions when Jeremy was bein' stingy with his money. Cassie even helped me when Jeremy DID give me money. Of course I wouldn't think she was rippin' me off or cuttin' me short!" Myron finally looked up from his notebook one last time. "Don't take it personal Berry, I'm just doin' my job." I brushed the hair out of my face that stuck to the sweat on my forhead and replied, "I know Myron and I do understand." At that time Myron closed his notebook and proceeded to tuck it in his leather planner. "Just one more quick question if you don't mind?" My mind and heart had just been put to ease when Myron asked me, "So, where were you last night and the day before around 3 a.m.?" Just as I was about to come out with my alibi, Damon yelled out the door, "C'mon man! Berry's been through a lot. Shit, we sat up 'til about 2:30 in the mornin' playin' Bid Whiz! Berry went to bed before me and woke up after me." Myrons' face frowned up. "Thanks for that info Damon, but I was talkin' to Berry!" Damon rolled his eyes into the back of his head like he was possessed and mumbled, "Dis nigga!" Myron rolled his eyes at Damon and waited for me to give account to my whereabouts on the nights in question. I repeated the same thing Damon said. "O.k. Berry. I'll be in contact if I need any more information from you. I guess you won't be needin' to go into hidin' now that both our suspects are deceased. Don't worry about Jeremy. He can stay in rehab until he completes the program. I'll definitely be keeping in touch with you. You still have my number? "Yes I do Myron. I called it today remember?" Myron smiled, "Yeah you did, didn't you?" Before Myron sat in the car and turned the key in the ignition, he yelled out the window to me, "If you hear anything Berry, call and let me know. Same goes for you Damon." Damon stood on the porch with his hands on his sides. Myron started the car. "Berry, don't make any plans to go out of state anytime soon. Make sure you call and check with me first if you do. Once we get this case closed you'll be free to enjoy that clean slate we spoke about a couple of days ago. I'll be in touch." Myron began to pull off in black the unmarked Lincoln car. Damon shouted from the top of the porch, "Hey Myron? Man, I thought we was goin' to the funeral home to pick up Tirianna's head stone?" Myron stopped in his tracks and yelled back at Damon, "Lynette picked ma up and they went about an hour ago!" Damon threw his hands in the air and replied, "So damn! I guess I wasn't gone find out until I sat here all day waitin' for you to interrogate Berry hunh? Myron pulled off in his indiscreet company car and drove down the street out of our sight.

"See Berry! You were all worried for nothin'. I told you

Devine and I had your back. How you digging that clean slate so far?" I sat just thinkin' about all the shit that had transpired over the course of my life. I just couldn't help but to wonder if it were all worth it. The money, clothes, jewelry, fresh rides.....WOW! Well.......at least I have a clean slate now to get my shit together. Now that Jeremy is gettin' cleaned out and neither of us have to be in protective custody, we can finally live the *normal* lives momma wanted us to live. I'm not sure about Jeremy or what his intentions are when he comes home, but I do know that I'm about to go to school and get some type of degree so I can take the money I have left and open my own business. Never thought about investin' in anything but material shit just so I could be the best dressed and have my own identity besides bein' referred to as Jeremy's *little* sister. Now I'm a grown woman with money to invest and a clean slate to finally jumpstart my life the right way......... but for some odd reason I can't help but to think to myself, How long will it last?"

About the Author

D'Aviér, poetess and published author of Poetic Expressions from the Soul, is a 3 time Editor's Choice Award winner and holds a gold medal of Poetic Excellence. She has been writing since the age of 8 and is one of Detroit's finest spoken word artists. She has performed her pieces at various venues throughout the city including Baker's Lounge, The Ribs & Soul Festival @Hart Plaza, Artist Village, Harbor House and Sweet Epiphany.

She refers to her talent as a "gift" from God and has worked with troubled teens using poetry as an alternative method of channeling aggression. Her company, *Poetic Expressions from the Soul LLC*, is registered in Detroit, Michigan and Alameda, California.

Her talent includes formerly co-hosting a weekly segment; "*Lyrically Speaking*," on Detroit Riot Radio (www.detroitriotradioonline.com) & currently working as a Special Correspondent on the HOTTEST show in the "D"; The *Video Shop* (aired on Comcast 68). Her poetry has also been featured in an upcoming movie; "*Chasing Normality*" filmed by WCT Entertainment.

Join D'Aviér on Face Book (www.facebook.com/davier1) or e-mail: davier_mammone@yahoo.com.

For booking information, contact Honey Management LLC: HoneyMgtllc@yahoo.com

www.ingramcontent.com/pod-product-compliance
Lightning Source LLC
Chambersburg PA
CBHW030502260626
47157CB00005B/1611